'Shhhhh . . .' Dermot moved his face towards her to kiss again. But then they could both hear footsteps coming up the staircase.

The footsteps paused in the hallway and a voice called over: 'Hey, Dermot, is that you?'

Dermot looked down, over Gina's shoulder, and saw the questioning grin of one of his school friends.

'Callum!' he called out. 'How's it going?'

At this, Gina turned. She saw a boy of about Dermot's age, seventeen, in jeans and a black leather jacket. His hair was jet black and casually spiky and he had a strikingly handsome, smooth-skinned face.

'You've got to be Gina,' he said with a little sideways smile and a raised eyebrow. 'I've heard a lot about you.'

Praise for the *Secrets at St Jude's* series:

'Warm-hearted and hugely entertaining'
Julia Eccleshare, Lovereading 4 Kids

'Raucous, hilarious and heart-warming . . . from one of the UK's bestselling authors of women's fiction. Packed full of friendship, fun, entertainment, love and hope'
Lovereading 4 Kids

www.rbooks.co.uk

Rebel Girl

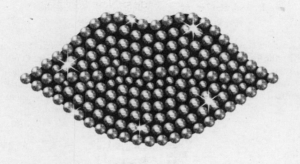

Carmen
Reid

CORGI BOOKS

SECRETS AT ST JUDE'S: REBEL GIRL
A CORGI BOOK 978 0 552 56122 8

First published in Great Britain by Corgi Books,
an imprint of Random House Children's Books,
A Random House Group Company

This edition published 2010

5 7 9 10 8 6 4

The Random House Group Limited supports The Forest Stewardship Council
(FSC®), the leading international forest certification organisation. Our books
carrying the FSC label are printed on FSC® certified paper. FSC is the only
forest certification scheme endorsed by the leading environmental
organisations, including Greenpeace. Our paper procurement policy can be
found at www.randomhouse.co.uk/environment

MIX
Paper from
responsible sources
FSC® C016897

Set in 12/16pt Minion by Falcon Oast Graphic Art Ltd

Corgi Books are published by Random House Children's Books,
61–63 Uxbridge Road, London W5 5SA

www.**kidsatrandomhouse**.co.uk
www.**randomhouse**.co.uk

Addresses for companies within The Random House Group Limited
can be found at: www.randomhouse.co.uk/offices.htm

THE RANDOM HOUSE GROUP Limited Reg. No. 954009

A CIP catalogue record for this book is available from the British Library.

Printed and bound by CPI Group (UK) Ltd, Croydon, CR0 4YY

MEET THE ST JUDE'S GIRLS ...

GINA

Full name: Gina Louise Winklemann-Peterson

Home: A fabulous white and glass, architect-designed beach house with pool on the Californian coast

Likes: Sunshine (sadly not often found in Edinburgh), swimming, Halloween, pointy ankle boots, Prada or anything Prada-esque, Reece's Pieces, her cell phone, her little brother Menzie (sometimes), coffee, a certain charming part-time waiter at the Arts Café called Dermot O'Hagan

Dislikes: Slithery octopus-type kisses, the totally gross sludge-green St Jude's school uniform, deadly dull history lessons, Charlie Fotherington-whatsit, boiled vegetables of any kind (I mean, guys, like, haven't you heard of stir-fry?)

Would like to be: A screenwriter – but absolutely no one in the whole world knows about that

Fascinating fact: Gina has three other best friends at her old school in California – Paula, Ria and Maddison. They still can't believe she goes to boarding school in Scotland

NIFFY

Full name: Luella Edith Millicent Pethurer Nairn-Bassett (no wonder she's called either 'Niffy' or 'Lou')

Home: The ancient, crumbling, ancestral mansion Blacklough Hall in Cumbria, England

Likes: Playing pranks, enormous horses and slobbery dogs, all team games, (especially hockey – she's really good), the St J's assembly game Banshee Buzzword Bingo (which she invented), her big brother Finn, the odd sneaked glass of expensive red wine, all school food, but especially pudding

Dislikes: Dresses, dressing up, poncy shoes and fussy clothes of any description, make-up, fussing with her hair, fussing about anything at all, her real name

Would like to be: A professional rider – an international show-jumper, or maybe a three-day eventer – that way she could do show jumping, dressage and her favourite, cross-country jumping

Fascinating fact: She can be fully dressed in all her riding clothes and hat in twenty-five seconds flat

MIN

Full name: Asimina Singupta

Home: A big family house with a huge garden in a suburb of Durban, South Africa

Likes: Running really, really fast and winning, being top of the class in every single subject, doing homework (it's so interesting when you really get into it), mango lassis, gold bracelets, reading science books, borrowing Amy's clothes, her mum's home-made curries

Dislikes: The sight of blood, Biology lessons, babysitting her little brothers and sisters, the food at St J's, wearing her hair in plaits, Scottish grey skies

Would like to be: A medical researcher or medical physicist. She has to do something medical because of her doctor parents but it can't involve blood!

Fascinating fact: Min's mother taught herself Italian and went all the way to Pisa to get her medical degree

AMY

Full name: Amy Margaret McCorquodale

Home: An amazing penthouse flat in Glasgow, Scotland, with a terrace and panoramic view of the city

Likes: Designer jeans (Iceberg), designer bags (Marc Jacobs), designer boots (Jimmy Choo, but only when her dad is feeling incredibly generous), Edinburgh's Harvey Nichols (obviously), very handsome boys, diamonds, champagne, dance music, dressing up and going out, her gran's mince and tatties

Dislikes: Penny Boswell-Hackett, Mrs Norah 'the Neb' Knebworth, everything in Niffy's wardrobe, French lessons, people teasing her about her Glaswegian accent, oh and Penny Boswell-Hackett (have you got that?)

Would like to be: Officially, she's going to do a law degree, then join her dad's nightclub business. Secretly, she'd like to be a famous and fabulous actress

Fascinating fact: Amy's mum and dad were teenagers when she . . . er . . . arrived. She was brought up by her dad, her gran and her grandpa. She hasn't seen her real mum for years

Chapter One

Long after midnight, Gina lay wide awake in her narrow dorm bed. It was her first night back at school after the Christmas holidays. Although the eighteen hours of travel which had taken her from California to her boarding school in Scotland had been exhausting, her body clock was still set stubbornly to Pacific Standard Time and she could not get to sleep.

She listened to the quiet breathing around her and guessed that the three girls who shared her dorm weren't having the same problem. Amy had travelled to St Jude's School for Girls in Edinburgh from her home just one hour away in Glasgow, so no jet-lag issues there. Niffy ('my real name's Luella, but it stinks') had come from the creaky, ramshackle family country home in Cumbria.

Then there was Min, who had flown into Edinburgh from South Africa earlier today, but the time difference between Scotland and her home town, Durban, was only a couple of hours, so she wasn't suffering.

The first night back at school was always weird.

The small room, the orange street-light shining behind the curtains, the narrow bed . . . everything felt so different from home. Even though Gina knew she would miss her family and the warm, outdoorsy Californian lifestyle, she was still pleased to be back. St Jude's was her school now and these three girls asleep in their beds beside her were best friends. Yes, she still had three best friends back home in California, but after two whole terms here, the St Jude's girls had become just as important to her now.

As Gina lay awake, looking up at the sloping attic ceiling above her head, she suddenly heard an unexpected noise. It sounded like the low rumble of a wooden window being pulled up, but she couldn't be sure.

The 'Iris' dorm, which Gina shared with Amy, Niffy and Min, was up on the top floor of one of the huge old Victorian houses which formed the St Jude's boarding house. Now that Gina was straining her ears, she thought she could hear more noises and they sounded as if they were coming from the top of the fire escape.

'Psssst! Are you awake?'

This whisper had come from Niffy's direction.

'Yeah,' Gina whispered back.

'Did you just hear that?' Niffy asked.

'Yeah.'

'It sounds like something's happening on the fire escape outside Daffodil dorm.'

Daffodil dorm, which Gina and her friends had shared last year, had four beds, just like Iris. It was also tucked up under the sloping attic ceilings. The great thing about Daffodil dorm was that it had a window leading out onto the fire escape. On a sunny evening, the top of the fire escape was a forbidden, but nonetheless delicious, place to sit.

'I think we should go and investigate,' Niffy added.

'I don't know,' Gina began. Wandering about the boarding house at night, for any purpose other than trips to the loo, was against the rules. She didn't like to think of herself as a total stickler for school rules, but she didn't like to break them unless there was a good reason.

'But what if someone has climbed up the fire escape and is trying to get in . . . ?' Niffy whispered urgently.

Gina considered: hadn't the noise sounded like a window being opened?

'What if some burglar or an armed maniac is trying to get into that dorm right now?' Niffy went on.

To be honest, if that was happening, Gina would really rather stay hidden in bed.

'We need to go!' Niffy said, throwing back her duvet and sitting up. She quickly pushed her feet into her slippers, then tied her dressing gown around her.

'Stay here if you like, chicken-licken, but I'm going to take a look.'

Gina sighed, pulled her own duvet back, then put on her slippers and dressing gown. She did not like the idea of confronting a burglar one tiny little bit, but she didn't like the idea of Niffy having to confront one on her own either.

'OK,' she agreed.

But Niffy was definitely going to go first.

The two girls tiptoeing out of the Iris dorm looked very different from one another. Gina was dainty, pretty, blonde and tanned. She was wrapped in a delicate silk kimono with fluffy pink mules on her feet. Niffy was tall, gangly, all arms, legs and unruly brown hair, bundled into some shabby brown tartan dressing gown, which had probably once belonged to her big brother.

Together, they crept out of the dorm, shutting the door quietly behind them. The hallway glowed faintly

4

with the night-lights which picked out the fire exits. Without hesitating, Niffy made straight for the door of the Daffodil dorm. She took hold of the handle and began to push the door open.

Gina stood behind her friend, her heart hammering nervously in her chest. She did not like this, not one little bit, but she couldn't stop herself from looking over Niffy's shoulder into the darkened room.

It was totally silent and still. Gina could make out the four beds in the room. Three girls, wrapped in duvets, seemed to be fast asleep. The window at the fire escape looked shut.

But then, all of a sudden, one of the duvet bundles sat up and hissed, 'Niffy! Is that you?'

'Yes,' Niffy answered.

The two other duvet bundles sat up too and someone snapped on a side light.

'For Pete's sake, go away!' the first bundle, now very obviously Milly from the Lower Sixth, instructed.

'Why?' Niffy asked, all fired up with curiosity.

'Go away!' Anthea, one of the other dorm members, repeated.

'No, she's OK, she can stay if she wants,' the third girl, Shyanne, chipped in.

'You know Gina, don't you?' Niffy asked as she

stepped into the dorm, revealing the friend standing behind her.

'Gina from California? Who goes out with Dermot at the Arts Café? Yup, we know her,' Shyanne replied.

'Hi,' Gina said shyly, not sure if she liked being known for just those two things.

'So what's going on?' Niffy wanted to know. 'We heard a noise . . . it woke us up. We thought you were being burgled or kidnapped – something exciting.'

Milly got out of bed. She was already wearing her dressing gown. 'Something exciting *is* about to happen,' she said. 'We just thought you were the Neb about to catch us red-handed.'

At this mention of the fearsome woman who ruled the boarding house, everyone felt a little shiver of nerves.

But nevertheless, Milly went over to the fire-escape window and threw it open, letting a blast of cold January air sweep through the room.

Anthea crouched down by the side of her bed and pulled out a neatly rolled coil of bright-blue climbing rope.

'If you're running away, you won't need a rope,' Niffy pointed out. 'There is a fire escape.'

'Very funny.'

'So what *are* you doing?' Niffy had to know, as two of the three older girls stepped out of the window, on to the top of the fire escape and began to tie the rope to the stair-rail.

'Shhhhh!' Milly insisted. 'What time is it?' she asked in a whisper.

Shyanne glanced at the clock beside her bed and whispered back, 'Twelve fifty-six.'

'Four minutes till delivery,' Milly said, 'and we've definitely put the hook end down in the garden, haven't we?'

As the girls checked over the rope arrangement, Gina and Niffy looked at one another.

What on earth was going on? Delivery of what?

'What's happening? C'mon. Give us a clue!' Niffy pleaded, determined to wangle something out of some-one. 'And where's Laurel?' she asked next, pointing at the empty bed. 'Broken something skiing?'

The two older girls came back in through the window and half closed it against the wind. They were obviously waiting for something to happen in the garden.

'Is someone coming? Is something arriving for you?' Niffy asked.

'Yes!' Milly said with exasperation. 'Just keep very quiet. At one a.m. exactly – I don't want to miss it.'

'And Laurel?' Niffy asked again in a tiny whisper.

For a moment no one replied. Gina bumped against Niffy's arm to try and give her the message to be quiet.

But then Anthea blurted out: 'Laurel's not here because her parents ran a building firm and it's finally gone bust. She was really worried about them last term and then, over Christmas, well . . . they told her they couldn't afford to send her back to St Jude's. So she's going to some day school in Aberdeen now.'

'That's tough,' Niffy whispered, shaking her head in sympathy. 'That is really tough. I spent half a term at a comprehensive last year and no one there was very pleased to see me.'

'Poor Laurel,' Gina sympathized. She had worries about family finances too. She knew her mom and her step dad, Mick, were hoping for a really big deal to come off for their software company.

As Gina's mom, Lorelei, had put it: 'Baby, if this happens, we won't need to worry about money for a while, just about making a great product. But if the deal doesn't go through . . . we might have to look at making some cut-backs.'

'It's one o'clock now,' Shyanne said, pointing at the bedside clock.

Milly pulled the window further open again and stuck her head out to listen.

The other girls in the dorm all crowded towards the window too.

There was definitely a sound coming from the garden . . . someone was down there and that someone seemed to be making a faint clinking noise.

Gina and Niffy looked at each other with raised eyebrows. Both suspected that the Daffodil dorm was about to get a delivery of bottles. Both guessed that there wasn't exactly going to be mineral water in those bottles.

In another bedroom, way over on the far side of the boarding house, but with a window facing onto the back garden, someone else was now waking up. Someone else who was also sure she had heard something in the garden.

This someone was definitely not going to be amused that bottles full of booze were being clinked in the St Jude's boarding-house garden at one o'clock in the morning on the first night of term.

Mrs Norah Knebworth, housemistress at the boarding house for seventeen years, opened her eyes.

She looked up at the ceiling of her small ground-floor bedroom and wondered what it was that had woken her. Once again, she heard some sort of unusual noise coming from the back garden.

She listened hard and then sat bolt upright. She was now certain that she had heard clinking: the unmistakable kind of clinking that bottles make when they bang together as someone tries to walk with them.

Bottles? *Bottles!!* Only one kind of bottle would be trying to make its way through the boarding-house garden well after midnight.

Mrs Knebworth raised her formidable bulk from the bed. Even in a ruffled pink and white nightie with a neat regiment of foam curlers organized through her steely blonde hair, she looked like a mighty force.

Putting her feet into sensible sheepskin slippers, designed to keep the chill of draughty Victorian floors at bay, she hurried over to her bedroom window. She peered through the chintz curtains and right there on the back lawn, underneath the long washing line where jeans and sweatshirts often flapped on breezy days, she saw something which made her mouth drop open with astonishment.

Not even ten metres from her bedroom window – the cheek of it! – was a teenage boy. In his hands was a large shopping bag, and attached to the bag was a length of rope.

Mrs Knebworth's beady blue eyes followed the rope up to the window at the top of the fire escape. There, in the dim light coming from the Daffodil dorm window, she could see two girls who were holding the other end of the rope.

This was just *unbelievable*!

Girls were trying to smuggle in booze, right under her very nose! How did they think they were going to get away with this?

Mrs Knebworth, who had grown up in Edinburgh's very respectable Morningside area, and who had never once even thought about breaking a school rule back in the days when she had been a St Jude's girl, was outraged. In fact, she was properly furious.

It wasn't just that these thoughtless girls in Daffodil dorm were in serious trouble; no, it was the fact that when things like this happened at the boarding house, it reflected very, very badly on Mrs Knebworth. And if stories like this got out into the wider community, well, they reflected very, very badly on the school.

She wasn't going to stand for that. Not for one moment.

Her fingers were at the window catch. She intended to throw the window open and bellow out into the garden: 'Hands up, you've all been caught!'

But she thought it through for a moment. The bag was still in the boy's hands. He would run off with it. The dorm window would shut, the lights would go off and everyone would deny everything. Even though she had seen it with her own eyes, she wouldn't be able to prove anything.

No. She wouldn't open the window and shout out, she had a better idea. Quickly pulling on her dressing gown, she decided to hurry as silently as she could up to the Daffodil dorm. That way she would catch everyone involved red-handed.

Mrs Knebworth sped out of her bedroom, past her small bathroom and through the private sitting room which she kept so neatly that whenever anyone was invited inside, they found it hard to believe that the housemistress really lived there.

Now she turned into a hallway and began to hurry down the long locker-lined corridor which connected this building to the second big house where, up in the attic, Daffodil dorm could be found.

Unfortunately, Daffodil dorm was many, many flights of stairs from the ground level and Mrs Knebworth was a large woman, approaching sixty, who had never been much of a keep-fit fan.

No matter how outraged and how furious she felt, she couldn't propel herself up the stairs as quickly as she would have liked.

But she was going to get there in time, she told herself as she pulled herself up the second flight by the wooden banister. She was going to catch them in the dorm with all their contraband, she thought, as her breathing grew a little wheezy on the third set of stairs. Oh yes, she was!

Chapter Two

Milly and Shyanne were taking the strain on the rope. They were tugging together, and slowly the heavy bag was starting to travel upwards.

'Why didn't he just come up the fire escape?' Niffy asked Anthea, who was standing beside her and Gina at the dorm door.

Anthea was holding the door slightly ajar, so that any strange or worrying sounds could be heard.

'Maybe he thought this would make less noise,' Gina whispered back.

'Then he should have wrapped those bottles up in tea towels,' Niffy replied. 'I'm surprised the whole blooming boarding house hasn't woken up.'

'Shhhh!' Gina urged, and for a moment everyone in the room froze.

Thud, thud, thud . . . It was faint. It was still far away

14

in the distance, but: *thud, thud, thud* . . . it definitely seemed to be getting closer.

'Someone's coming up the stairs!' Niffy exclaimed. 'QUICK!!'

Milly and Shyanne yanked at the rope, then Milly reached over and grabbed hold of the bag. 'RUN!' she hissed at the boy and waved her arms about to give him the idea.

Thud, thud, thud . . . There was no doubt that the footsteps were growing closer, and every one of the girls had a horrible feeling that there was only one person in the boarding house who had such a heavy tread.

Shyanne and Milly hurried back in through the window and pulled it shut behind them. Anthea ran over and snatched the bag from Milly's hands. It was packed with a jumble of goodies, but it was immediately obvious that three bottles just visible from the top had to be dealt with immediately.

Anthea grabbed hold of the bottles and looked frantically around the dorm for a hiding place.

Thud, thud, thud . . .

If this really was Mrs Knebworth – the Neb – then she was just seconds from bursting through the fire door at the top of the final set of stairs.

'Give them to us!' Niffy instructed.

Anthea ran over and handed the bottles, not to Niffy, who was still holding the door open, but to an astonished Gina.

Gina almost let them slip from her hands with fright. Why was she being landed with this? She was the one who had wanted to stay in bed and keep out of it all.

She didn't need to be told what to do though: she fled from the scene, straight to her dorm and jumped into bed, taking the two bottles of wine and one of cider with her. Then she lay there, *terrified*, wondering what was going to happen next.

Niffy tried to escape too. She let go of the door, turned on her heel and ran after Gina towards the Iris dorm. But right behind her, she heard the horrible screech of the fire door opening on its spring-loaded hinges, then the outraged voice of the Neb called after her: 'Luella Nairn-Bassett, just where do you think you're going?!'

Niffy froze.

The Daffodil dorm door banged shut, and the faint light visible underneath it went out.

Niffy turned and faced the Neb in the dim light of the hallway.

'You will come with me into Daffodil dorm and you will all tell me just exactly what has been going on up here,' Mrs Knebworth hissed furiously, her pink quilted dressing gown and foam curlers not diminishing her many terrifying qualities in the slightest.

Even in this light, Niffy was sure she could see the steely blue gaze coming from the Neb's narrowed eyes.

This was one of the rare occasions in Niffy's life when she couldn't immediately think of anything to say. Niffy had been at boarding school since she was eleven and she'd grown up with a prank-playing big brother, so she was usually very, very good at inventive excuses, brilliant tricks and spectacularly good fibs. But here in the hallway at 1 a.m. with a furious Mrs K facing her, Niffy's mind went stubbornly blank.

For a moment, she wondered if she should say this was nothing to do with her – she'd just got up because she'd heard a noise.

But she had a feeling Mrs Knebworth wouldn't believe her.

The housemistress reached for the Daffodil dorm door handle. 'Follow me,' she barked at Niffy.

The dorm was in darkness with the three girls in bed, just like it had been when Niffy had opened the door earlier. But Mrs Knebworth was not in the mood for any pretence; she reached up and snapped on the overhead light.

Suddenly Daffodil dorm, with its gaudy new pink and yellow wallpaper, was starkly visible.

'Get up!' Mrs Knebworth commanded. 'Don't even pretend for one moment that you're not awake!'

Reluctantly Milly, Anthea and Shyanne sat up in their beds and looked at the housemistress nervously.

'Where is that bag?' Mrs Knebworth snapped. 'Don't bother denying it; I saw a boy out in the garden with a bag not three minutes ago.'

She walked over to the window and threw it open. The blue rope was still hanging from the rail of the fire escape.

'This was the pulley, so where is the bag?' the Neb demanded.

She turned and faced them, crossed her strong arms under her terrifying bosom and stared her frosty, furious stare at each of the four girls in the room in turn.

'Aha!'

One of her hands shot out and she pointed at the incriminating item. She'd spotted it badly hidden under Milly's bed.

Without any hesitation, she marched over and pulled it out.

'Right, what have we got here?'

She yanked the bag up, placed it on Milly's bed and began to examine the contents.

She unpacked one small bunch of pink roses, a box of chocolates, a jar of strawberry jam and a paper bag which turned out to contain three chocolate croissants.

'Where's the contraband?' the Neb demanded. 'I heard the clinking of bottles when this bag was being lifted up. And I think we all know exactly what that means.'

'No, there weren't any bottles,' Milly insisted. 'It was a friend of mine . . . my boyfriend, in fact . . . and he was just trying to be romantic.'

'Ha!' Mrs Knebworth spluttered. 'No one goes to this much trouble for *romance*. The sooner you girls find that out, the better. You were smuggling in booze. I know it. I heard it. Now, open up your chests of drawers while I search the cupboard.'

Niffy stood very still beside the dorm door, wishing that she'd not got involved with this. It so wasn't worth it. The only thing inside that shopper that was of any interest to her right now was the bag of croissants. She wouldn't mind snaffling a couple of those and then heading quietly back to bed.

But she had a feeling the Neb was not going to leave without a very, very big fuss. Look at the bossy old battle-axe, rifling through drawers, searching under beds and all through the cupboard. Bent double over the drawer at the bottom of the wardrobe, Mrs Knebworth in her quilted dressing gown looked like a baby-pink, over-upholstered sofa.

After a long and full search of every nook and cranny in the dorm, the Neb finally had to admit that she was not going to unearth any offending bottles.

She got up from her knees, dusted herself down and told the dorm furiously, 'Don't think for one moment that I'm going to leave it here! So far, I've only found chocolates, flowers and pastries. But I saw the boy, I heard the clinking! And when I find the bottles . . . Oh yes, I will find them, mark my words, then you will be in such trouble, you won't know what's hit you. In the meantime' – Mrs Knebworth's eyes narrowed and she looked at each face in turn – 'you are all gated for three weekends.'

Chapter Three

The terrible, piercing wail of the boarding-house siren tore through Iris dorm at 7.30 the next morning. It was so loud and so unexpected that Amy and Min both jumped out of their beds feeling panicked. But after the adventures of the night before, Niffy and Gina found it much harder to get up, despite the terrible racket blasting from the speakers in the hall.

All four girls headed for the big, communal bathroom to splash warm water on their sleepy faces – Niffy and Min – or cleanse, tone and moisturise – Amy and Gina.

Then drawers were opened, backs were modestly turned and the four climbed into the clean and folded St Jude's uniforms which had been untouched for the three weeks of the Christmas holidays.

No school uniform could ever be lovely, but the St Jude's uniform was particularly disgusting. For a start, it was green. Not bottle green or army green, but somewhere sludgy between the two. There was a baggy, pleated skirt, which only looked reasonable if it was several sizes too small. Then there was a cardigan, which again had to be worn shrunken if you didn't want to look like a librarian.

A boring white shirt and either green tights (yuck) or green woollen socks (yeurrrrgh) completed the look.

Both Niffy and Amy, who had been at St Jude's since they were eleven years old, looked at home in their well-worn uniforms. Min and Gina's skirts and cardigans still looked too big and too neat. So Gina rolled up the waistband of her skirt to shorten it and pushed her knee socks down to mid-calf. At least that way she exposed some tanned Californian leg and didn't look like a total nerd. She also messed up her blonde hair a bit and fixed a glittery clip into it. There were no boys at St Jude's so it wasn't worth applying make-up and going all out, but Gina still wanted to look cool.

Amy, fully dressed now, pulled open her bottom drawer to get her school shoes and was astonished to see two bottles of wine and a bottle of cider lying in there.

'There's three bottles of booze in my drawer!' she exclaimed. 'Who put those in there?!'

Gina and Niffy exchanged a guilty look.

'Sorry,' Gina began. 'Niffy and I got caught up in this thing with the Daffodil dorm last night and . . .'

'What thing?' Amy asked. She sat down on her bed, tossed her blonde hair over her shoulders and set her pretty face to quizzical. 'Last night? When? In the middle of the night? Why didn't you wake us?'

Min shook her head. 'Don't think I'd have wanted to get involved.'

'What happened?' Amy persisted.

'Believe me, you were better off in bed,' Niffy said.

She and Gina gave their friends a quick update on last night's events.

'The Neb's on the warpath, she knows these bottles are somewhere – and you've put them in *my* drawer!' Amy spluttered when she'd heard enough. 'Thanks a lot!'

'Well, she couldn't risk putting them in your suitcase, Min,' Niffy chipped in, 'in case of the stowaway spiders. Black widows . . . button spiders, violin spiders . . . I know just what can come back in luggage from South Africa.'

'Nif!' Min protested. 'That was two whole years ago,

and it was a harmless house spider, just a bit bigger than the ones you're used to.' But she was laughing at the memory. Niffy had screamed the dorm down and brought Mrs K running when a very dozy, squashed black insect had crawled from Min's suitcase at the start of her second term.

'Uhhhh!' Niffy shuddered at the memory. She was an outdoorsy, adventurous type, but big fat hairy spiders . . . they were her weakness.

'You weren't involved, Amy, so I thought she wouldn't look in here,' Gina justified herself. 'I wasn't trying to get you in trouble or anything.'

'Our first night back,' Min sighed, 'and you're already in trouble.'

For a moment, Niffy looked annoyed. How typical of goody-two-shoes Min. Min was never, ever in trouble, of course. There she was, hair all neatly brushed and held back with a school hairband, skirt the exact regulation length, earrings the correct tiny little studs. Min had probably done extra homework during the holidays.

'Swot!' Niffy said, but she shot Min a smile before adding gloomily, 'Even though the Neb didn't find the booze, me and the Daffodils are gated for three weekends.'

24

'Unbelievable!' Amy said. 'So just how are you planning to get to your hockey training sessions?'

Niffy, who had been chosen to play in the Scottish Under-Seventeen team, gave a shrug.

'Hopeless, totally hopeless,' came Amy's response. 'Well' – she turned her attention back to the three bottles – 'we can't have the booze anywhere in this room. As soon as we set off for school, you can bet the Neb will be up here combing through our cupboards and our drawers like a demon. No sooner do we step out of this building than she will be searching high and low for that stuff. Sit,' she instructed her friends, 'and think! Where in this building will she *not* look?'

For several moments, they sat in silence, then their thoughts were interrupted once again with the terrible wail of the siren calling them to breakfast.

'I've got it!' Amy exclaimed, jumping from her bed. She wrapped the bottles in a hand towel and headed out of the dorm with a curious Niffy hot on her heels.

In the big bathroom – empty now, as almost everyone was heading downstairs to the dining room – she stepped into a toilet cubicle, carefully set her towel package down on the floor, then lifted the lid of the cistern.

'Hold,' she instructed Niffy, handing her the porcelain lid.

The toilets were old-fashioned, from the Seventies or Eighties, with deep, water-filled tanks. So Amy could easily slide one of the wine bottles down into the water. Then she pulled the flush, just to make sure that everything still worked as usual.

She replaced the lid and told her friend, 'One down, two to go.'

'Genius!' Niffy replied.

'Gated on your very first evening . . . that should be a record, except last term Gina was gated as soon as she set foot inside the building,' Min reminded them.

'Yup,' Gina confirmed.

The four friends were walking together along the path which connected the boarding house to the main St Jude's school building. Lots of other boarders in school coats and woolly hats were hurrying along the same path as well. It was only a five minute walk, but in the raw January weather, it still felt too long.

There were never more than about a hundred boarders at St Jude's. The rest of the school was made up of day pupils. Every day, from every corner of Edinburgh and its surrounding towns, three hundred day girls filed into the imposing three-storey stone building of the senior school.

'Did you see Angus at Christmas?' Amy asked Niffy, so unexpectedly that Niffy blushed a frantic shade of pink.

'No!' came the surprised reply.

'No?' Amy asked. 'Why not? I thought you two were mad about each other. I thought the only thing that was keeping you apart was the fact that unfortunately he'd gone on a French exchange programme.'

'Huh!' Niffy said, and didn't look as if she was going to offer any more information, so Gina stepped in.

'What's up?' she asked. 'I thought you guys were going to try and get together in the holidays?'

'He was only home for a week, so he stayed with his parents and didn't come to see his aunt and uncle – or me – because apparently he didn't have time,' Niffy declared huffily.

'Oh,' Amy said carefully, because she knew just how close Niffy and Angus had been last year.

Angus was Niffy's first ever boyfriend. He was a friend of her brother's and a great guy. Amy didn't think he was the kind of person who would hurt Niffy's feelings deliberately.

'What do you think?' Amy ventured. 'Is he still in touch?'

'He emails and he still phones once in a while . . . but it seems a bit . . . vague,' Niffy decided.

'Oh . . .' Amy said.

The four girls walked along in a tactful silence for a few moments, then suddenly Niffy burst out with, 'I bet he's met some glamorous French girl! I bet that's what it is. I mean . . . French girls? You know how sexy and generally gorgeous they are. I bet he's snuggled up with some Solange or Celestine.'

'Don't be nuts!' Gina said with a giggle. 'He'd have told you, he's a very nice guy.'

'Maybe too nice to tell me . . .' Niffy huffed.

'You could be sexy and glamorous too, Niff, if you put your mind to it. I mean, the next time you see him, you could be totally transformed.'

Amy was getting that glint of enthusiasm in her eyes. There was nothing she liked more than to glamorize her friends with all her expensive make-up and very lovely clothes. Although she didn't as a rule lend much to Niffy, because her friend was just so careless and clumsy.

'A great haircut, Niff, some nice new clothes, accessories, jewellery, just a touch of make-up,' she went on. 'You know that you scrub up very well. We've done it before. You don't have to spend a lot, you could go to somewhere like . . .'

Amy paused for a moment. She wasn't really up on where was cool on the high street; she only liked to shop in designer boutiques and Harvey Nichols.

'River Island,' she suggested, trying not to shudder too much at the thought.

'Huh?' Niffy humpfed. 'New clothes? New hair? Jewellery? Not bloody likely. Have you heard how much pocket money I'm getting this term? Thirty quid. Thirty quid for the whole term! The Nairn-Bassett finances are even more up the creek than usual. Finn and I each got a new pair of wellies for Christmas.'

There was an awkward silence as the three other girls thought of their Christmas presents. Amy's and Gina's parents were loaded and Christmas Day had been one long, delightful unwrapping session: new clothes, new shoes, new gadgets, all kinds of lovely treats. Min's Christmas had been more restrained, but only because her parents had five children, so they couldn't go completely over the top.

Still, Min had got a brand new laboratory-standard microscope which she knew had not been cheap.

'That's a shame, Niff,' Amy said finally, 'but you know

you can always borrow our stuff. You just have to ask. There's not any real money problem at home, is there?' she asked gently.

Niffy just shrugged and said, 'No worse than usual.'

'You wouldn't be able to go out shopping and have your hair cut anyway,' Min pointed out. 'You're gated.'

'Oh yeah,' Niffy remembered.

'It's only three weeks until the Mocks,' Min said, reminding them all about the upcoming trial-run exams. 'Mrs K doesn't let people go out at the weekends before exams, unless they've got a very good reason.'

'Oh no!' Gina protested. 'So just how am I supposed to see Dermot?'

Chapter Four

'*Bien, mes amies!*' Madame Bensimon, the French teacher, exclaimed. '*Vous devez travailler, travailler, travailler.*'

Work, work, work.

This was the first time Gina had experienced St Jude's in the run-up to exams. And if this was how intense it was going to be for *mock* exams, what on earth was it going to be like when it came to the real thing?

This was only their second day back, and so far every single teacher had laid out a structured revision plan. The amount of homework and studying ahead looked absolutely mountainous. All Gina's evenings and her entire weekends looked as if they were going to be totally filled up with studying.

'*Ré-viii-sion,*' Madame Bensimon said in French.

There was extra revision homework, special revision timetables, even long lists of revision vocab. In fact, if

Gina heard the word 'revision' again, she was going to scream!

'So that long email you were reading and re-reading in the study last night, was that from Dermot by any chance?' Amy murmured the question very quietly into her friend's ear.

'Maybe,' Gina whispered back.

Dermot had been Gina's boyfriend for . . . almost seven months now. Seven months! That was ages. Gina had never gone out with anyone for such a long time before. But then, it wasn't as if they saw each other every day or even every week, so maybe that's why they were still so interested in each other.

Anyway, Dermot was like a best friend: a really, really nice, really good-looking best friend. Gina found it almost as easy to talk to him as to kiss him.

'He's got mock Highers next month,' Gina whispered back to Amy, 'so he's working really hard and he doesn't think we'll be able to go out for weeks.'

'Boo-hoo,' Amy commiserated.

'He said I can still go to the café and see him,' Gina added. Every Saturday, Dermot worked in his dad's café as a waiter; that was how Gina and her friends had got to know him in the first place. 'If we're allowed to go,' she concluded gloomily.

'Trust me, I will get us out of the boarding house for a few hours on a Saturday at least, but a trip to the café isn't the same as a nice, fun date though, is it?' Amy replied.

'And what about you? Any news?' Gina asked.

Last term, Amy had started to go out with Niffy's big brother, Finn, but this had caused a huge meltdown between Niffy and Amy. The arguments had gone on for weeks until finally Amy and Finn had promised to call everything off until the Christmas holidays.

'Later,' Amy hissed, pointing a finger briefly at Niffy, who was sitting on the other side of Gina.

'*Silence!*' Madame Bensimon glared at them both, putting an end to the conversation.

'Ailsa.' The teacher gestured to one of the girls seated at the side of the room. '*C'est très chic!*' was her comment. Madame, who was something of a *très chic* French lady herself, couldn't help noticing major style changes.

'Ah . . . *merci*,' Ailsa said with an embarrassed smile.

Now everyone was looking at Ailsa, whose straight golden hair had been cut into a really short bob. For a St Jude's girl, short hair was unusual. Most of the girls preferred long hair, shoulder-length at the very least.

Niffy glanced over and saw the new style. Ailsa looked so different, so completely transformed, that even Niffy, who didn't usually notice haircuts or new clothes, couldn't help being impressed.

'That *is* nice,' she whispered to Gina.

'Mmmmm . . .' Gina agreed, although she would sooner cut off her hand than lop off any more than the bi-annual two-centimetre trim from her own long, blonde mane.

'*Ré-viii-sion*,' Madame repeated. 'Have we made up timetables? Have we considered how we will cover all the necessary subjects before the exam which you will sit in exactly nineteen days?'

It was unusual to hear Madame Bensimon speak English; she almost always spoke French in class. But this was obviously so serious a subject, Madame didn't want to risk a misunderstanding.

Several members of the class, including Min, looked panicked by the news that the exams were only nineteen days away.

'Madame?'

One of the day girls, Penny Boswell-Hackett, raised her hand to ask a question.

'Here we go,' Amy couldn't help whispering under her breath.

Amy and Penny had history.

They had fallen out on Amy's first day at St Jude's,

four years ago, and it didn't look as if they were going to make up any time soon.

Penny Boswell-Hackett was clever, reasonably pretty and very, very old-school Edinburgh posh. Her mother had gone to St J's, her grandmother had gone to St J's, probably even her great-grandmother too. This made her think she was totally superior and oh-so-much-better than girls like Amy.

Amy was also clever, pretty and just as good on the hockey pitch as Penny would ever be. But Amy wasn't from Edinburgh; she was from Glasgow. Amy didn't have several generations of St Jude's educated ancestors; she had a single dad, who'd grown up in a council tower block. Penny spoke with a posh and cultivated voice; Amy had a strong Glaswegian accent.

Basically Penny was far too much of a snob to ever be able to overlook any of these things and see Amy as an equal.

No, Penny B-H and her best friends, Tiggy and Louisa, forever known by Amy and her friends as Piggy and Weasel, were always, always going to look down their pointy little noses at Amy and whoever chose to be her friend.

'Tiggy, Louisa and I have got this plan,' Penny told Madame Bensimon with a smug smile. 'We're going to go round to each other's houses and revise for two hours and then have a little treat afterwards. Maybe go out for a hot chocolate, or give each other a manicure or do our hair. You know, so we've got something to look forward to afterwards. So it's not just all work, work, drudge, drudge.'

Madame Bensimon gave a little clap, she was so captivated by this idea.

'*Bien sûr*,' she said. 'A little reward. *Mo-tee-vah-sion. Quelle bonne idée!*' Then she gave Penny, her favoured star pupil, a special little smile of appreciation. 'You are going to do very well in your French exam, Penelope.'

Amy couldn't stop a little snort of exasperation escaping from her nose. The Penny and Madame Bensimon love-in just wound her up every single time.

Even more annoying was the fact that Penny's idea was good. Amy could imagine her and Gina studying for two hours and then enjoying a little pampering treat afterwards. It would be fun. But now, of course, she couldn't do anything like it, because Penny would accuse her of copying. Argh! The thought!

'*Une bonne idée*,' Madame Bensimon repeated. 'Maybe we can all plan a little revision time with our frrrriends and a spoiling "*petit rien*" afterwards.'

'Well, except for the poor boarding-house girls,' Penny pointed out cattily. 'They can't leave the building after school, except at weekends, so no going out for hot chocolates for them. Poor little boarders, nothing to do every evening except swot.'

'Oh, shut up!' Amy hissed.

Chapter Five

Dinner in the boarding-house dining room was always noisy. Ninety or so girls fought for space at the long tables that had been set out in the room. The junior girls were always to-ing and fro-ing from the serving hatch with dishes, courses and fresh jugs of water. The level of chat rang all the way up to the ceiling and the Neb often had to stand up at her little table in the bay window at the top of the room and ring her bell several times to ask for peace and quiet.

There was always talk: about school, about home, about news and, best of all, gossip. Every little snippet of exciting information was picked apart with relish.

'So you've been gated along with Daffodil dorm – how come?' one older girl was asking Niffy.

'Ermmm . . .' Niffy quickly stuffed a great forkful of shepherd's pie into her mouth so she wouldn't have to answer this immediately.

'Something about a delivery . . . in the middle of the night? Was it Milly's new boyfriend?' the other girl wheedled, desperate for more information. 'Apparently he is absolutely gorgeous.'

Niffy chewed slowly; she didn't like this sixth former much and didn't really want to share any private information with her. Plus, she could see other curious heads turning in their direction, desperate to listen in.

Luckily the Neb's little bell began to ting-ting-ting-a-ling for silence.

'Girrrrrls,' she began pleasantly, then ran through some housekeeping pointers before turning to the guest she had sitting with her at the top table.

'Now, you may be wondering who I have sitting up here with me this evening . . .'

Every head and neck craned in the direction of the table. A pale and dainty woman of about thirty or so sat beside Mrs K. She had long, totally straight brown hair which fell down her back from a centre parting. The most striking thing about her face was how pale and totally plain it looked.

She was wearing an olive-green cardigan buttoned up to the neck.

Mrs Knebworth, with her bouffant blonde hairdo

and purple satin blouse, looked almost glamorous by comparison.

'OMG, do you think it's the Neb's daughter?' Amy whispered.

Mrs Knebworth often spoke about her one and only daughter and there were many photos dotted about her private sitting room. But only a handful of boarders had ever managed to meet her.

'I thought she was blonde,' Niffy whispered back.

'I'd like you all to say a big hello to Alison McKinnon, Miss McKinnon to you, of course. She's going to be the assistant housemistress here and a great help to me. She comes to us all the way from the island of Barra, and she's very much looking forward to getting to know you all and finding her way around her new home and Edinburgh. I hope you'll all make her feel very welcome.'

Everyone clapped politely, then Mrs Knebworth sat down and the level of chat, clatter and noise immediately returned to normal.

'An assistant housemistress?' Min queried. 'We've only ever had Mrs Knebworth, plus the cook.'

'Perhaps it's new regulations,' Gina wondered. 'With ninety kids, you might have to have more adults around.'

'Maybe Mrs K's planning to take a bit more time off during term time,' Niffy pondered. 'I mean, usually she never leaves the place except during school hours.'

'From Barra?' Amy repeated, her nose wrinkled up. 'Bound to be a total country bumpkin. You'll get on well.' She directed this last bit at Niffy.

'Shut up!' Niffy said cheerfully, before adding the sarcastic comment, 'We can't all come from the glittering glamour of *Glasgae*, you know.'

'Hey!' Shyanne from Daffodil dorm leaned back in her chair so she could talk to Niffy behind the backs of the four girls between them. 'Did you find a good hiding place?' she asked, referring to the three bottles.

'Yup,' Niffy confirmed.

'One of us will have to contact you about that in the near future,' Shyanne added, putting a code voice on a little thickly.

'The mission awaits command,' Niffy teased.

'Whatever!' Shyanne said and snapped her chair back into place.

'You need to get rid of that stuff before you get into any more trouble,' Min chipped in, having overheard Shyanne, 'and why is Laurel missing from their dorm?'

'Oh, haven't you heard?' Niffy asked. She was scraping

the last of the first course from her plate and was now looking over towards the serving counter to see what was coming up for pudding. 'Apple sponge with custard, excellent,' she said, mainly to herself.

'Laurel?' Min reminded her.

As Niffy began to tell how Laurel had left school because her parents had lost their business, she realized that everyone around her, including Amy, was listening in with widened eyes.

'Poor Laurel,' Min sympathized.

Everyone who heard the story looked sorry. Every girl knew that it was expensive to be at St Jude's. They were all here because someone was paying the substantial fees, and being at the boarding house cost three times more than going to the day school. In the back of most girls' minds was the usually unspoken fear that if the family's money suddenly ran out, they would have to leave the school and all their friends, possibly very abruptly.

'Are all *your* families OK?' Amy asked her friends. 'I mean . . . loads of businesses are having a rough time right now.'

Gina was the first to quietly admit, 'My mom and Mick are stressed out about whether or not they're going to land some big software contract. I think, if they get it, they're going to be great. But it's a big deal. They're going to hear real soon.'

Amy looked at Min next, who replied with a shrug, 'People need doctors, no matter what. So my mum and dad feel lucky – everything's fine with them.'

'Just like my dad,' Amy said with a smile. 'He has eleven nightclubs now and he says everyone needs to go out, have a drink, have a dance and forget about their problems, no matter how bad it gets out there.'

There was a little pause. Niffy had already told them things were worse than ever with the Nairn-Bassett family. Niffy came from one of those ludicrously posh families where all the money was made generations ago and now it was just trickling down and slowly but surely running out.

The Nairn-Bassetts lived in a vast country house which was in serious danger of collapsing because it was in such a bad state of repair. But there was no money in the N-B family to pay for any of the work which needed to be done. Mr N-B ran the estate around the house in a vague and half-hearted way.

'Well, you know my dad . . . he sells barley and a few cattle,' Niffy said through her large mouthful of sponge and custard. 'No one ever seems to pay him very much for it. Mainly we sell stuff out of the house.'

'Huh?' Gina asked.

'You know, paintings, silver coffee pots, the odd bit of jewellery . . . Dad takes it off to Sotheby's in Edinburgh and usually gets five thousand pounds a pop. My ancestors bought some classy items, you know.'

Amy listened to this with wide eyes. 'So they're stripping the place out, but they still won't think of selling it?' she asked. 'That house must be worth a fortune! Why don't they just sell it to some Norwegian millionaire or something and live happily on the proceeds for ever, especially now that your mum's been ill.'

Niffy was just as wide-eyed back. 'You don't understand, Amy,' she replied. 'The Nairn-Bassetts have had Blacklough Hall for eight generations. My parents aren't going to be the ones to sell it. They're just hoping that something happens, fortunes change . . . I dunno . . . they're just . . .'

'Hanging on for a miracle,' Amy said bleakly.

'I keep telling you, I'm going to be a world-famous—'

'Show-jumper and solve all their problems.' Amy finished Niffy's sentence and rolled her eyes.

'Three-day-eventer,' Niffy corrected her.

'Oh yes, let me go through the list of world-famous, multi-millionaire, three-day-eventers I know,' came the sarcastic reply.

'Ooooh, it's the little Irises, are we having a fight?'

All four dorm girls looked round to see Mel crouching down beside Amy's chair.

Mel was the Lower Sixth girl who liked to think of herself as the boarding-house wild child and sexpert. Her hair was bleach-blonde and elaborately styled, her eyeliner was dark and shiny and this evening her shirt was unbuttoned low enough to reveal a black lace bra, while the denim miniskirt beneath it was barely long enough to cover her knickers now that she was crouched down beside them.

'Are you going out somewhere?' Amy asked.

'No. Just trying out a few new things, perfecting the Mel Wintertastic look.'

'You're obviously expecting a heat wave this January, are you?' Niffy had to ask.

Mel ignored this and carried on with her own line of questioning: 'So, tell me your news. How were the Christmas hollies? What did we get up to? How many fabulous new boys did we meet? Not as many as Mel, I don't think.'

Amy snorted at this.

'Did Amy get back together with Niffy's brother, Finn? That's my number one question,' Mel said.

'Mind your own beeswax,' came the sharp reply from Amy.

'Oooooh, I'll take that as a "no" then, shall I?'

Amy made no reply.

Niffy quickly looked down at her plate and spooned up another mouthful. She didn't even want to hear this conversation. It was still a sensitive subject.

Mel turned to Gina. 'Please tell me that at least all is well with you and the sweet little waiter from the Arts Café?'

'Yeah, all is well,' Gina confirmed.

'Seeing him this weekend?' Mel asked curiously.

'Well . . . I don't know yet. He's really busy studying for his Highers so I'm not going to see so much of him. He's got Mocks, just like us, and then in the summer he sits the real thing. He's trying to do well enough to get into Edinburgh University.'

'Oh dear.' Mel gave a roll of her eyes. 'Then it will be goodbye Gina and hello to unlimited Uni totty. I've seen it so many, many times before,' she said in a totally infuriating superior way.

'That's not very nice, Mel.' Gina wanted to defend

Dermot against this horrible accusation, but she didn't really feel as if she could.

Dermot going to university felt like an age away, but she couldn't promise that he wasn't going to dump her. Not now or in a few months' time or whenever . . .

'Poor Gina.' Mel sighed, although she didn't sound in the least bit sympathetic. 'Maybe you should dump the soon-to-be-uni boy before he dumps you. Believe me, it's always better to be the one doing the dumping. Definitely.'

Chapter Six

'Just what exactly is that?' Amy wanted to know when she spotted a large cardboard box underneath the boarding-house mail table as she and Niffy arrived back from school several days later.

Amy bent down to have a closer look at the box and turned to Niffy with surprise: 'It's got your name on it! Are you expecting a parcel?'

'Really?'

Niffy sounded casual.

She sounded too casual, in fact. Amy knew at once that something interesting must be going on because this was Niffy's way of trying to play it down.

'I think my mum might have sent me some new hockey boots. My old ones are a size too small and they're falling apart.'

'Hockey boots? In a box that size?' Amy looked at her friend suspiciously.

'You know what mail order companies are like . . .' Niffy picked up the box and began to head towards her locker with it. 'The boots are probably inside three layers of cardboard in there.' She opened the door of her long, metal locker and began to stuff the box into the narrow space.

'Aren't you going to open it?' Amy asked.

'Nah . . . it's boring, honestly,' Niffy assured her, applying the force required to squeeze the box into the locker.

'I'll do it later. Right now, I need tea and I need cake.'

Then from her skirt pocket, she brought out her locker key, which was attached to some gruesome little hairy haggis key ring.

Now this was unusual, Amy couldn't help thinking. Niffy usually just banged her locker door shut and left it unlocked.

'Why are you locking your door?' she asked her.

'Oh . . . well . . .' Niffy put the key back into her pocket and began to walk jauntily down the corridor towards the kitchen, 'they're brand-new boots, Aim, my mum would kill me if they went off for a walk on their own.'

*

49

Min was in the boarding-house study room staring at a computer screen in horror. Right in front of her eyes were the current entry requirements for the university she was aiming to get into when she left St Jude's: Cambridge.

Yes, it was still two years or so before she could even think about filling in the application form, but right here was proof that she would have to do incredibly well not just in her Advanced Highers, but also in her Highers and the Standard Grades she was going to sit this summer.

Good grief. Nothing but a long line of As and starred As was going to do.

Min gave a deep sigh and sank her face into her hands for a moment. But that just upset her even more, because now she could feel all those soft bumpy spots that had broken out all along the sides of her face.

Eeek!

She pulled her long hair down around her cheeks to cover the offending breakout. This was just horrible: she'd always been so proud of her lovely smooth skin. She was just about to Google 'spots' and 'treatment of' when she thought about the other thing she'd been meaning to do when she'd sat down here at the row of terminals in the study.

Greg.

Super-nice Greg Riley – who she'd met via an online physics club. Super-nice Greg who'd helped her so much with her biology ... who'd taken her on two dates last term . . . whose mum was a bio-chemist who believed in healthy eating and had given him two brown paper bags of homemade popcorn to take to the cinema. Super-nice Greg, who'd kissed her under the mistletoe at Christmas!

Ooooh ... just thinking about the mistletoe moment made blood rush around her system in all sorts of strange and tingly ways. Min was a highly intelligent girl; she knew these feelings had nothing to do with butterflies.

Greg had emailed all through the holidays, just as he'd said he would, and he'd already asked what she was doing this weekend and could she pencil a slot into her revision timetable to see him?

That was the problem.

There wasn't going to be any time in her life to see him. She was going to have to study every waking hour until the Mocks and then, as soon as they were over, she was going to study every waking hour until the real thing.

It was the only way to secure the Cambridge-worthy results.

How else could she possibly get a string of As if not by studying *all* the time?

Greg was super-nice. But she had to think about Cambridge. Focus on Cambridge. It was what she and, above all, her mum and dad, desperately wanted for her.

Min opened up a new message and began to type:

'*Hi, Greg, Hope you're good. I have soooooo much work on. It is only 16 days till my first exam. I can't believe it. Scary!*'

Min paused. She wasn't sure how to put this next bit. She really, really liked Greg. He was so into all the same things that she was and he was totally nice and cute too. But they'd only actually kissed once – well, maybe two or three times on that same day. So did that technically make him a boyfriend? Did Min actually have to finish with him? Or could she just say '*See you soon*' in a vague kind of way and hope that he understood?

And then there were the spots. Greg hadn't seen her spots. They hadn't been there before Christmas. She didn't think she wanted him to see them. They were so grubby-looking and so embarrassing.

'*I know I can't see you before the Mocks,*' she typed. '*I just won't have time. I'm not sure how much time I will have after the Mocks. I have to do really, really well in these exams. I'm aiming to get an A in everything. I know you are too, so I know you'll understand.'*

She paused again and wondered how to sign off. *Love?* NO! *Yours?* No. *See you?* Well . . . considering she wasn't going to see him, that wouldn't be right.

'*Very best wishes, Min.'*

She quickly typed in two kisses then scrunched up her eyes and hit Send before she could even think about reading it again and changing her mind.

Then she sat looking at the screen and felt a wave of panic. What would he say? Was this really a good idea? Wasn't she just going to regret this? Wouldn't it be nice to see him again?

She flicked back to the Cambridge University entry requirements page again and tried to focus on it. This was what she wanted to do. This was where she wanted to go. This was much more important than Greg . . . wasn't it?

She flicked back to her inbox again. No reply. She stared at the inbox, willing Greg to be reading her note and to be thinking of a way they could get through all their work and still be friends. Be slightly more than friends.

When the ping of incoming mail went off, Min gave a little jump of surprise. Yes! It was from Greg.

Her fingers suddenly felt a little unsteady as she moved towards the keys that would open up the message.

But then there it was before her. Just the very brief:

'*Oh, I see. G x*'

Min's face was in her hands again.

This just didn't feel as if it was what she really wanted.

Chapter Seven

'Girls! Three of you! This is too much! I can't take it!'

'Shut up, Dermot!' Amy told Gina's boyfriend playfully.

Dermot O'Hagan was such a teaser; he had to be told to shut up regularly and in Amy's opinion Gina didn't do it nearly enough.

Dermot was manning the counter in the stylish first-floor Arts Café this morning, maybe because his dad wasn't around. Usually on a Saturday, Dermot was head waiter, bustling about the tables in his uniform consisting of a bright-blue shirt, dark trousers and an apron.

'Hey, Gina,' he said, his eyes lighting up and a grin splitting his face at the sight of her.

'Hey, Dermot,' she replied, smiling straight back.

He ducked briefly out from behind the counter to plant a quick kiss on Gina's mouth.

'Welcome back to bonnie Scotland. More kissing later . . .' he told her, fixing his blue eyes on hers. For a moment such an intense look passed between them that it felt as if everyone and everything else had stopped in its tracks. The two of them were just so happy to be together again.

'OK, you two . . .' Amy said, breaking the spell.

'Amy, nice to see you.' Dermot turned and gave her a smile, then he paused, not able to remember for a moment who the third girl with them was.

'Rosie,' Amy reminded him, 'from the year below us.'

'Hi!' Dermot said cheerily. 'Sorry, I've had a caffeine overdose this morning, brain not working properly, liable to collapse any moment. If I do, just shove a chocolate brownie in my mouth, that usually works.'

The girls giggled in response to this.

He hurried back behind the counter: 'Now, it's two grande lattes with super-skinny-skim,' he remembered for Gina and Amy. 'Rosie, my dear, what is your preferred poison?'

Once Rosie had placed her order, Dermot busied himself with the coffee machine, but he still wanted to know: 'So, where are Min and the Nifster? Why are they not with you on the first Saturday outing of the term?'

Gina began the explanation. 'Min is studying, because you know, we all have these tests for the first two weeks in February. And Min is convinced she's going to flunk out unless she studies for ten hours a day,' Gina added, with a roll of her eyes.

'Flunk out?' Dermot asked with a grin. 'I like that.'

'Yeah, fail, whatever you guys call it. And because of studying, by the way, we're only allowed out on Saturdays . . . and only if we're very, very nice to Mrs K.'

'And Niffy?' Dermot reminded her.

Amy chipped in with the answer to this question.

'Niff has managed to get herself, and very nearly Gina, gated for at least three weekends.'

'Really? Exciting story?' Dermot wondered.

Amy nodded. 'Oh yes, it involved a love-struck boy wandering about the gardens at night with a bag full of wine, jam and croissants.'

'What?!' Dermot laughed.

'Not love-struck for Niffy,' Amy added. 'I think she was just there for the croissants. But anyway . . . she's gated, the wine is dotted about toilet cisterns all over the boarding house and what more can I say?'

Dermot laughed again. 'Never a dull moment.'

He put the drinks in front of them, took their money and told them, 'I can't wait to hear more.'

But now there were other customers waiting at the counter, so the girls knew to go and take a seat. Dermot would come over and chat to them when he could.

As they made for a table, Rosie couldn't help saying with a little sigh, 'He is so cute and so funny – I wish I had a Dermot.'

'Hands off!' Gina said immediately.

Rosie winked at her, then as they settled into their seats, she turned to Amy and asked, 'So are you finally going to tell us all about Finn, or what?'

Amy leaned back in her chair, put her mug of coffee to her lips and took a little sip before finally answering. 'Well . . . the truth about Finn is that there's nothing to tell. Three whole weeks of the Christmas holidays went by and I didn't go down to Niffy's place. Neither of them came over to Glasgow to see me. We were all "too busy", or maybe it was all too awkward. So there you go . . . '

She sipped calmly from her coffee cup again.

'But,' Gina protested, 'you must have phoned? Or mailed? Or *something*?'

'Yeah, well . . . there was a bit of that, but it's just

friendly. There's nothing romantic going on,' Amy admitted.

'He phones you and you just chat . . . like friends?' Rosie wanted to make sure she'd understood this properly. 'You and Finn, who last term were *panting* at the thought of each other?'

'Positively *drooling* all over each other,' Gina added.

'Stop it!' Amy complained. 'He sounded strange on the phone. Maybe Niffy was listening in on his calls. She always talked to me when he'd finished. I really, really like Finn,' she admitted with a sigh. 'There. I've said it. But neither of us wants to upset Niffy like we did last term. That was terrible. Really just bogging awful. So I'm just leaving it as it is and we'll see. Maybe something will change . . . in a bit.'

'Really?' Gina wasn't so sure. 'You're just going to wait and see?'

'Really,' Amy confirmed.

'Have you talked to Niffy lately? Do you know what she thinks now?' Gina asked.

'No. I don't want to stir it all up again,' Amy said. 'Now . . . how do we feel about blueberry muffins?' she asked, desperate for a change of subject.

'We feel generally quite positive,' was Gina's reply.

'Yes,' Rosie agreed, 'we do.'

'So if I went up there and got a blueberry muffin, you two would share it with me?' Amy asked.

'Yeah,' Gina and Rosie both agreed, then as Amy left the table, they gave each other a little look. Amy had been weird about food last term, going for entire days sometimes without eating anything, but it was all supposed to be sorted now. If she wanted to eat one third of a blueberry muffin as a little mid-morning treat, they knew they should encourage her. It was a good thing.

When Amy came back with the muffin, she brought Dermot along with her.

'Five minutes off for good behaviour,' he said, pointing to the assistant who had taken over behind the counter.

'Where's your dad today?' Gina asked as Dermot slid down onto the sofa beside her, wrapped his arm round her waist and pulled her in for a kiss.

'He's still in bed. Heavy night for him last night, I think, he's not going to come in until later.'

'Oh. So, no non-café based dates for us until . . .'

'Until July,' Dermot said, his face so dead-pan it wasn't obvious if he was joking or not.

Gina looked at him. 'You're kidding, right? No dates till July means I may have to find someone else to take me on dates.'

'Gina, you wouldn't do that to me!' Dermot protested.

'Yes, I would!' she insisted, but playfully.

'You're not allowed out on Sundays, I have to work Saturdays and study on Sundays . . . we are doomed,' he teased.

'Totally!'

He squeezed her hands in his. 'Don't say that.'

His eyes were looking at hers all serious now.

Then she voiced the thought which had been on her mind ever since Mel had mentioned it: 'Aren't you just going to finish with me when you get to university anyway?'

She didn't mean it to sound at all heavy, but somehow it did.

'Gina!' Dermot protested.

He glanced over to the café counter. The queue was small and moving steadily through the capable hands of his dad's assistant.

'C'mon, let's go out into the hallway and talk . . . See you in a minute,' he told Amy and Rosie.

Gina followed Dermot out of the café's main double

doors. The Arts Café was a large, modern space above a lively modern art gallery.

Out through the doors was a white hallway with a lift, and wide stairs leading both up and down.

Dermot led Gina up a step or two, just so they were out of the way of the doors and the lift.

Then he wrapped his arms round her again and pulled her in for the proper 'hello and welcome back from the holidays' kiss he'd been longing to give her since she'd set foot inside the café.

Now that Gina had his familiar arms round her waist, his face against hers, his eyes looking into hers, she remembered with a tingle of excitement how much she really, really liked him.

'Hey, you,' she said, before moving her mouth towards him. His lips brushed against hers.

Then they were kissing, properly: her eyes shut, concentrating on nothing but the connection, the very close and tight connection between them. He tasted of the coffees he'd gulped down this morning: warm and a little earthy. Funny how when they'd started the kiss they'd almost seemed a little out of practice. Their noses had bumped together.

But now, as their lips touched and their tongues

moved around, it seemed practised and delicious and perfect.

Once she started kissing Dermot, Gina never felt as if she wanted to stop. Ever. He pulled her in tightly, moving his hands up her back.

'Missed you . . . missed you a lot,' he said when they finally broke off.

'I can't just see you at the café,' she complained.

'Shhhhh . . .' Dermot moved his face towards her to kiss again. But then they could both hear footsteps coming up the staircase.

The footsteps paused in the hallway and a voice called over: 'Hey, Dermot, is that you?'

Dermot looked down, over Gina's shoulder, and saw the questioning grin of one of his school friends.

'Callum!' he called out. 'How's it going?'

At this, Gina turned. She saw a boy of about Dermot's age, seventeen, in jeans and a black leather jacket. His hair was jet black and casually spiky and he had a strikingly handsome, smooth-skinned face.

'You've got to be Gina,' he said with a little sideways smile and a raised eyebrow. 'I've heard a lot about you.'

'Yeah . . .' Gina said, feeling a little unprepared. Although she really wanted to meet some of Dermot's friends, he hadn't said anything about this happening today.

'Gina, this is Callum Cormack, he's in the same year as me. In fact, he's doing all the same classes as me . . . in fact, I would even go so far as to call him a friend,' Dermot laughed. He came down off the stairs and smacked Callum on the back. Then he pulled open the café door and suggested they all go back in.

'Are you sure?' Callum asked. 'I feel as if I've interrupted something a little juicy.'

'No, c'mon in with us,' Dermot insisted.

'Very, very nice to finally meet you,' Callum said to Gina and held out his hand for her to shake.

As she took it and said 'hi', she felt as if she was being scrutinized just a little too closely.

Callum followed her and Dermot over to the table where Rosie and Amy were deep in conversation. Once Callum had been introduced, he pulled up a chair, and after Dermot had sorted his friend out with a coffee, a busy half an hour or so passed.

Amy and Gina asked Callum all sorts of embarrassing and revealing questions about Dermot. Dermot, who now had to wait tables, kept flitting in and out of the conversation, his ears burning.

'My favourite book is not *Winnie the Pooh*! What on

earth are you telling them? No, I do not like *High School Musical*! Shut up!!' was one of Dermot's interruptions. 'And anyway, what about you? You had an emo phase last term. You even wore *eyeliner.*'

'Did not!' Callum pretended to be outraged.

The girls found the teasing going on between the two boys very funny.

'Do you want to know something very, very interesting about Dermot?' Callum turned to Gina and asked.

'Yeah,' she answered, still giggling.

He gestured for her to move much closer . . . closer still. When he cupped his hand over his mouth, she understood that Callum wanted to whisper in her ear. So she leaned the side of her head towards his face.

'Dermot . . .' Callum began in a whisper.

Suddenly Gina felt a little too aware of how close Callum was. She could smell the clean, soapy waft of boy toiletries coming from him.

She looked at his hair, slightly damp with gel, and the smooth skin on the stretch of cheek beside his ear.

'Dermot . . .' Callum repeated, 'has boxer shorts with the Simpsons on them.'

'And socks,' Gina said. She didn't know if either of these things was true, but she didn't want Callum to feel that he knew Dermot oh-so-much better than she did.

'Sorry to break up the party, but we really have to go,' Amy announced. She tapped at her dainty watch. 'It's nearly twelve thirty. We have to be back to the boarding house for lunch and then there's no going out again until next Saturday!' she added gloomily.

'Is it boarding school you go to, or is it prison?' Callum asked.

'We'd probably have more fun in prison,' Amy replied.

As soon as the girls had said their goodbyes and were out of the café, they all wanted to gossip about Dermot's friend.

'He was very funny,' Rosie spoke first.

'And cute,' Amy pointed out.

'Yeah,' Gina added, 'so if anyone happens to be interested, I could ask Dermot to bring him along the next time we go to the café,' she suggested.

'You want to watch yourself there, Gina,' Amy chipped in. 'As far as I could see, the only person Callum really seemed to be interested in was . . . you.'

Chapter Eight

By the time Gina, Amy and Rosie were at the bottom of Bute Gardens, it was three minutes to one and the lunch bell.

'We have to run!' Rosie urged the other two, because being late was awkward. Being even a few minutes late meant all sorts of disapproving looks from the Neb and filling in special forms and having a little red mark placed against your name, and if you earned two of them, you lost one evening pass. And so on.

'Run!' Rosie urged her friends again.

Amy and Gina upped their speed to a sort of enthusiastic jog, because they were both wearing tight, heeled boots.

As they approached the boarding house, Niffy's head appeared from an upper window and she shouted out a countdown: 'Fifty-nine seconds till the bell . . . fifty-six, fifty-five, fifty-four . . .'

This gave the three joggers the encouragement needed to speed them up and send them hurtling into the front door with just thirteen seconds to spare.

As they went panting into the sitting room to sign in, they saw that Mrs Knebworth was not there.

Usually at crucial signing-in moments, the Neb loved to lord it over the signing-in sheets, her watch raised up to her face, noting the exact lateness of everyone who came in after the curfew.

'Hello . . . just in time,' Miss McKinnon said pleasantly. She was sitting on the sofa with a newspaper in her hands. 'Have you had a nice morning?'

'Yes,' Amy answered, sounding almost surprised at this burst of niceness. Then the siren went off, alerting everyone to Saturday lunch and making any further conversation impossible.

As soon as Niffy caught sight of her friends, she broke the news that everyone else who had been in the boarding house that morning was bursting to discuss.

'Have you heard?!' Niffy hissed, as everyone scraped chairs and took their places at the dining tables.

'What?' Amy asked.

'The Neb has gone out . . .'

'On a Saturday?' Gina broke in. This was big enough news in itself.

The Neb was such an in-built part of the boarding house it was hard to imagine the building even existing without her. She obviously had to leave the house during term time, but it never, ever seemed to be when the girls were actually there.

'Not only that' – Niffy paused and let a grin break out across her face. This news was just too good to be true, she was going to relish every moment of sharing the information – 'but she was picked up in . . . a blue Jaguar . . . by . . .' She paused, loving the way that every face was hanging on her every word, '. . . a man!'

Before anyone could spoil the gossip, Niffy quickly added, 'And don't worry, I have personally interviewed every single girl who saw this man and no, he was not young enough to be her nephew or her daughter's boyfriend or anything like that. He looked a bit older than the Neb, apparently, and they were both very pleased to see each other.'

'Did they kiss?' Amy wanted to know straight away, although she was pulling a face at the thought of anyone wanting *voluntarily* to kiss the Neb.

'Haven't been able to establish that,' Niffy said.

'Reports are mixed. Some claim there was a cheek-on-cheek moment, some say a brief hug. But there was definitely enthusiastic physical contact of some kind.'

'Gross!' was Gina's verdict on this.

'So is that why your head was poking out of Rosie's dorm window?' Amy now understood.

'Totally,' Niffy confirmed, scooping a big forkful of beans and sausage into her mouth.

'You wanted to see for yourself?' Amy asked.

'Yup. Soon as I've finished here, I'm going back to my post. Unfortunately I can't stay after two thirty this afternoon, so I was hoping you would volunteer.'

'What's happening after two thirty?' Gina wanted to know.

'I'm going off to my hockey training.'

'Thought you were gated,' Min chipped in.

'Yeah, well, but apparently you can still attend official school business while gated.'

'Thought hockey training didn't start till four?' Amy asked next.

'Shhhhhh,' Niffy warned her; she didn't want this to be widely known. 'Miss McKinnon doesn't know that though, does she?'

Amy looked up at her friend in surprise. 'So what are you planning to do out there on the streets of Edinburgh for ninety minutes in your school uniform with your hockey kit on your back?'

Niffy just tapped the side of her long nose. 'Mind your own beeswax,' she replied.

'I will not!' Amy said angrily.

'I have an appointment. It's nothing dodgy, it's perfectly normal and fine but I just want it to be a surprise. That's all.'

It didn't matter how many wheedling questions Amy, Gina or Min asked after that, Niffy refused to tell them anything more. She said that when she got home from hockey, everything would be revealed. Once they'd finished lunch, however, she did persuade them all to come up to Rosie's dorm, along with Rosie, to do a Mrs Knebworth watch.

'Miss McKinnon said she expected her back some time after lunch,' Niffy told them, her face pressed right up against the window.

'Maybe they went out for lunch,' Gina suggested. She was perched on the end of Rosie's bed, along with Min. Neither of them was half as interested in seeing Mrs Knebworth's lunch-date as Niffy, Rosie and Amy were.

Amy had pulled a chair up to the window so she could chat and be comfortable without losing sight of the driveway for a moment.

'So the car pulled right in to the drive down there?' she just wanted to establish.

Niffy nodded; she was concentrating intensely on the street leading up to the boarding house.

'Blue car approaching!' she called out. 'Action stations!'

Now Gina and Min couldn't resist coming to the window as well.

'Pull back!' Niffy warned them. 'They're not going to do anything interesting if there's a crowd.'

Everyone stood about a metre back from the window. Fortunately it was a wide Victorian bay window with plenty of room for everyone to still get a look.

The blue Jaguar indicated and turned into the driveway.

'It's them!' Niffy hissed. 'It's got to be.'

The car drew smoothly to a stop. For a moment or so nothing happened.

'If they're kissing, they're kissing in the car,' Amy decided.

'No . . . no . . . wait . . . what have we here?' Niffy asked.

The driver's door opened and a man in a suit and tie stepped out. He walked round the bonnet and then went to open the passenger's door.

'Oh! He's opening the door for her! That is so sweet,' Gina couldn't help adding.

'She's stepping out . . .' Rosie said in a whisper. 'He's offering her his arm . . . they are walking towards the steps.'

All craned their necks so they could look down. The steps were beneath them and had a very inconvenient roof.

'Was that . . . ?'

'Did he . . . ?'

'Awwwww . . .'

'I think . . .'

Not one of the five had been able to get a clear view of what had happened. The heads had seemed to turn towards each other and pull a little closer, but because of the little roof above the staircase, it had been impossible to tell what had happened next.

The pair could have kissed or they could just have turned to smile at each other. Mrs Knebworth could have been involved in full-on mouth-on-mouth action! But the girls were never going to know.

'OK, next time she goes out with him, we have to make friends with the Lower Fives in Poppy dorm. They have a bay window with a side view. Mrs K's snogathon will not escape us from there,' Amy said.

'Why don't we go down to the little kitchen and make tea? Maybe she'll want a cup after all that kissing . . .'

'Eeeeeuwwwww,' Gina squeaked.

'Maybe we can find out more!'.

Chapter Nine

'You know, if Mrs Knebworth wants to date someone, it's kinda interesting but it's not soooo interesting that I need to sneak downstairs and start spying on her,' Gina told her friends with a shrug of her shoulders.

'I agree,' said Min.

'But you two don't really understand,' Amy protested. 'We've known the Neb since we were eleven years old and she's never even left the boarding house at the weekend before, except to go to church. This is completely bizarre.'

'Whatever.' Gina gave another shrug. 'I need to try and call my mom . . . I still haven't heard from her. I thought she would have called by now . . .' Just the slightest flicker of worry travelled across her face as she said these words.

'The big deal?' Amy remembered.

'Yeah. I thought they were going to hear on Friday, but there's been no word.'

'Maybe they're celebrating?' Amy wondered.

'You and Niffy can go down and wind Mrs Knebworth up if you like, but I'm going back to the study,' Min declared.

'Suit yourself,' Niffy replied. 'C'mon, Amy . . . you go ahead, there's just something I need to fetch first. To make sure I can still get out at two thirty . . .'

'Huh?' Amy asked, but Niffy was already heading out of the door.

When Niffy arrived at the little kitchenette beside the dining room, where girls were allowed to make tea and toast in between meals, Amy was already there waiting for the kettle to come to the boil.

'Is she about?' Niffy whispered to Amy.

'In her sitting room,' Amy murmured back.

Niffy stepped out into the hallway and listened.

The door to Mrs Knebworth's sitting room was shut, but she could hear voices. Miss McKinnon must be in there with the Neb.

'Anyone like a cup of tea?' she called out cheerily in the direction of the closed sitting-room door.

The voices stopped for a moment.

Then Miss McKinnon replied, 'Yes, that would be very kind. Two white teas, one with a sugar.'

'Coming right up,' Niffy replied.

'Quick,' she hissed at Amy as she came back into the kitchenette, 'you make the tea. I'll add the surprise.'

'What?!' Amy asked, as Niffy pulled a packet out of her trouser pocket.

'Wait and see,' came Niffy's instruction.

Amy poured boiling water onto teabags in the two mugs she'd prepared, stirred in milk, then fished the bags out and flicked them into the swing top bin.

Meanwhile, Niffy emptied most of the contents of the sugar bowl into a mug and sprinkled the white powder from her sachet over the rest.

'You're not going to poison the Neb, are you?' Amy asked cautiously. 'Not even a bit.'

'No!' Niffy protested. 'This is just for fun.'

She shot Amy a wink.

As Niffy tried to put the empty powder sachet in the bin, Amy managed to snatch it out of her hands.

'Aha,' she said, reading the instructions before Niffy could snatch it back. 'I saw the boots you were playing in yesterday afternoon,' she added.

'What?' Niffy looked confused now.

'You were playing hockey in your old boots

yesterday. Not shiny new ones. This packet comes from the box in your locker, doesn't it? You've got *plans*, haven't you?'

'She gated me for three whole weekends,' Niffy said. 'She has to expect a little bit of rebellion in return.'

'What else is in that box?' Amy wanted to know. 'I hope you've got something much more exciting than trick sugar.'

'Shhhhh!' Niffy instructed, and picked the mugs up with one hand and the sugar bowl with the other.

'Niff, how are you going to get out at two thirty now that the Neb's back? She'll know there's no hockey till four.'

'Shhhhh!' Niffy repeated.

She walked over to Mrs Knebworth's sitting-room door and pushed it open with her shoulder.

The Neb was sitting in one of the armchairs and Miss McKinnon was perched on the edge of the sofa beside her, as if she didn't intend to stay in the room for long.

'Hello, Mrs K,' Niffy said with a smile. 'It's so unusual to see you going out in the middle of the day.'

'Oh! Well, just lunch . . . lunch with an old friend. Relative, really. No, I suppose a friend . . .'

She seemed a little flustered. She lifted her glasses

away from her face and rubbed at her eyes before she settled the specs back in place.

'Here we go.' Niffy handed Miss McKinnon her mug of tea, then gave Mrs Knebworth hers.

Niffy held out the sugar bowl to the housemistress, who loaded up her teaspoon and sprinkled sugar over the hot liquid.

Amy, standing watching at the doorway, held her breath.

As soon as the powder hit the steaming tea, it began to fizz, froth and bubble. Foam began to rise up in the mug, then gush down the sides. Boiling hot, foamy tea was dripping all over Mrs Knebworth's skirt before she had time to react.

'Good grief!' she exclaimed loudly, jumping up from her seat.

This immediately brought a small group of girls who'd been passing to the open sitting-room door.

'What on earth is going on?' the Neb demanded, holding the foaming mug well away from her. But it still spluttered and fizzed, sending more tea onto the carpet now.

'Why has my tea gone mad?' she asked, causing the girls at the door to giggle.

'Don't just stand there goggling!' she told them off.

79

'Go and get some cloths. Now! This is my best skirt. Luella! What has happened to my tea? This has to have something to do with you.'

The stern face was once again turned in Niffy's direction, but this time Niffy was prepared.

'No idea,' she replied with the wide-eyed look which she used to get away with just about everything. 'Maybe the milk's off and something in the sugar has reacted to it.'

'Ha!' Mrs Knebworth was totally unconvinced. 'In all my years of drinking tea, milk has never reacted with sugar to make a mess like this.'

She gave Niffy another long, appraising glare. 'If you're up to something, I will find out about it,' she added.

Niffy was tempted to say: 'You haven't found those bottles yet, have you?'

But she knew that might be extremely dangerous. She might end up being gated for the whole term.

Amy and the other girls came in with cloths and paper towels they'd found in the kitchen.

'If you would be so kind as to clean up the tea on the carpet,' the Neb said, setting the frothing mug down on a side table. 'I'll have to go and change.'

'Ermmm . . . Miss McKinnon, I know I should stay

and help clean up,' Niffy said quietly, so she couldn't be overheard by the Neb, 'but I have to head out to my hockey practice, remember? I told you . . . and that other . . . appointment.'

Amy glanced up, wondering what Niffy was up to now.

'Oh yes,' Miss McKinnon recalled. Glancing at her watch, she added, 'You better hurry along. You don't want to be late.'

Chapter Ten

It was just a few minutes before supper time on that same Saturday, when Min looked up from an intense burst of chemistry revision and spotted Gina bent over her desk in the study room. Min decided to pack away her books for now and go over to speak to her friend.

'Hi, Gina,' she whispered, 'I didn't know you were in here.'

'I know, I'm following your good example,' Gina said proudly.

'Impressive,' Min whispered back. There was a handful of other, older girls in the study, so they had to keep very quiet. 'Have you spoken to your mum yet? Is everything OK?'

'Yeah!' Gina replied with a grin. 'I finally spoke with them about an hour ago. Everything's great. They got the deal!' At this, Gina mouthed the word 'Yeaaaaay!' and punched the air with her fist.

'Is it a really good one?' Min asked.

'Well, let's just say they were still in bed, sleeping off a big celebration.'

'That's really, really great news, Gina,' Min told her.

One of the older girls looked up and cleared her throat in a way which made Min and Gina realize they had to stop talking.

'Supper?' Min asked in the tiniest whisper possible.

Gina nodded, but as she began to pack away her stuff, they both spotted Amy walking into the study.

Amy went to the row of computers, picked a chair, sat down and began to log on.

'Checking email?' Gina said beneath her breath. 'Let's go over.'

So Min and Gina tiptoed across the quiet room, to let their friend know they were there.

As they got to Amy's chair, she was already calling up her mail, clicking through the junk, looking for the interesting messages.

Turning to see her friends, she whispered a tiny: 'Hi.'

Min and Gina stood behind her; it was just a moment or two before the supper bell would ring so they thought they might as well wait for her.

Amy was reading through an email long enough to

cover half the screen when all of a sudden, she gasped.

'Oh no!' she exclaimed, loudly enough to cause every head in the room to look up.

'What's the matter?'

'What's up?'

Concerned, Gina and Min both spoke together.

'Oh no!' Amy repeated. She leaned in towards the screen and seemed to begin reading the email again. As if she wanted to be sure of the contents.

'This can't be happening,' she whispered. 'I can't believe it . . .'

She turned to her friends and they saw the look of horror on her face.

'Amy?'

'What?' both asked.

'Read it, just have a read . . .' she instructed her friends, then she got up from her chair and began to hurry towards the door.

For a moment, Min and Gina were torn.

Should they follow her?

Should they read the email first?

'Read it first.' Min made the decision. 'We'll be able to help her better.'

Both girls bent over the screen and raced through the message, which was from Amy's dad.

Although they weren't familiar with some of the financial terms, they both understood the general drift pretty quickly.

Amy's dad's nightclub business was in serious trouble. One of his business partners had racked up a huge debt and now most of the business would have to be sold off to pay the debt back.

Call me as soon as you get this, princess, [the message had ended]. I want to explain it to you properly. I'm going to come and see you as soon as I can. And please, try not to worry. It's a big thing, but we can deal with it. OK.

Loads of love,

Dad.

Min and Gina both looked at one another.

'That's terrible,' Min said.

'Let's go find her,' Gina replied as she closed down Amy's email, sure that she wouldn't want anyone else to read this.

Just then the supper siren blasted through the study room and as Min and Gina went out into the corridor, the first person they ran slap bang into was Niffy. She was in muddy and damp hockey kit, slightly out of breath as if she'd had to run to get back in time and she still had her kit bag over her shoulder.

'Hi!' Niffy called out.

'Have you seen Amy?' Gina asked.

Niffy shook her head.

'We have to find her,' Min said urgently.

But now the corridor was filling up with girls coming from every corner of the boarding house and heading towards the dining room.

'We'll try the dorm,' Gina said.

Both Min and a sweaty, panting Niffy followed Gina down the corridor against the crowd of girls moving in the other direction.

'What's the matter?' Niffy wanted to know.

As they headed up the flights of stairs towards the attic, Min and Gina gave Niffy the details of the email.

'You have got to be joking!' was Niffy's reaction. 'Her dad? The nightclub business? I thought everything was fine. Didn't Amy say that just the other day?'

'I know,' Min agreed. 'She looked totally shocked.'

'I think it's a complete surprise to her dad as well,' Gina added.

As they rounded the next corner, to mount the final

flight of stairs, they saw Amy coming down the stairs towards them. Her face looked pale and strained, as if she was working hard to hold herself together.

'Amy!' Niffy was the first to speak. 'I'm so sorry. We're all so sorry about what's happened.'

Amy put her hand over her mouth and gave a wide-eyed gasp. Her eyes filled up with tears and she looked as if she was struggling not to cry.

'I don't know the full story yet,' she blurted out in a wobbly voice. 'Maybe it's not as bad as it sounds. I'll have to call him . . . I'll speak to him after supper. Maybe I'll call him now . . . I won't be missed at supper . . .'

But when she saw the anxious looks on the three faces, she quickly added, 'No, it's OK, I'll come to supper. I know how much you'll worry about me if I miss a meal.'

Stepping down to their level, she gratefully accepted the hugs and the pats on the back that they all wanted to give her.

'Your dad's a really good businessman,' Gina reminded her. 'He'll figure something out.'

'You're right,' Amy said, and wiped her eyes with the back of her hand.

'You'll feel better once you've had something to eat,' Niffy told her. 'I know I always do.'

'Niffy!' Amy was suddenly staring at her friend with a look of absolute horror across her face.

'NIFFY!' she repeated.

Gina and Min were now looking at Niffy too, mouths opening in astonishment.

'You've cut off all your hair!' Amy said, although now that everyone was looking at Niffy properly, this was totally, stark-staringly obvious.

Chapter Eleven

In the Daffodil dorm that night, long after lights out, it was hard to fall asleep. Each of the dorm girls lay very still in their beds and thought about a whole list of worrying developments.

Amy stared at the ceiling and thought about her dad. He was going to come to Edinburgh to see her next weekend. She had managed to speak to him not long before bedtime and he'd told her not to panic: 'All businesses go through ups and downs,' he'd said. 'We have to keep calm and not do anything stupid. It's important to think hard together before we act.'

But Amy lay there in the dark, and she was panicking. What if they lost their home? What if he lost all his nightclubs and didn't have a business left? What if . . . ? She could feel tears drip from her eyes into her hair as she let herself think about this. What if she had to leave St Jude's?

It did happen.

It happened more often than anyone liked to think about. What about Laurel in the dorm next door? She'd had to leave all of a sudden. Imagine if Amy had to do the same thing?

In the bed next to Amy's, Niffy was also awake and thinking exactly the same thing. What if Amy had to leave? What if Amy wasn't going to be at St Jude's any more? And what about Amy's stressful relationship with food? Niffy had noticed that Amy had hardly eaten a thing at supper. This was what had happened last term – Amy had stressed out about things and her eating had got totally messed up. They were all going to have to look after Amy carefully and make sure that it didn't happen again.

As if this wasn't enough to worry about, Niffy also moved her hand up to her head and felt the raw ends of her hair.

Raw . . . that was how the ends felt. As if they were broken off and supersensitive, like nails that had been bitten too deep.

Despite the very kind comments that her friends had made as soon as they'd spotted the dramatic haircut, Niffy now had the feeling that she'd made a terrible mistake.

'It's sooooo short!' Gina had marvelled. She'd had to walk all round Niffy, to take in the bare ears and the exposed pale neck.

'What do you think?' Niffy had pressed her for an opinion.

'Wow!' Gina had said. 'It's so daring. A real boy's cut.'

'You don't think it's too frizzy at the front?' Niffy had worried.

'I'm sure there's something you could put in it, to calm it down,' Amy had suggested.

'You cut off all your hair?' Min had gasped. As she took in Niffy's hairstyle, she'd held her own long, inky locks in her hands, as if she'd been worried that someone was going to sneak up and cut hers off too.

'It's very sporty,' Gina had added. 'Think how easy it will be to wash and dry.'

'Hmmm . . .' Niffy had agreed, only too aware that no one had told her it looked good.

'Do *you* like it, Amy?' she had asked her oldest friend directly. 'Do you think it looks good?'

Amy had looked back at her and said nothing for a few moments. Then she'd finally answered: 'I'm going to have to stare at you for the rest of the evening and just try and get used to it. Ask me later.'

That was when Niffy knew she'd made a mistake.

She'd gone to a barber's shop. One with a sign outside which promised: ALL CUTS £8. That had fitted with her frugal budget. So she'd walked in as she'd planned, cool as a cucumber, and asked if she would be able to get a 'short back and sides'.

The barber had raised his eyebrows and asked her several times if she was sure.

'Yeah, yeah. Definitely,' she'd insisted, then she'd settled herself into the chair and the barber had bunched all her hair together into a hand-held pony tail at the back and just chopped it all off in a single whack. Ouch. It had almost physically hurt as the hair had hit the floor.

For the next thirty minutes or so, Niffy had felt incredibly daring and excited as the barber had worked over her head. She'd felt the scissors move up above her ear lobes, much higher than she'd ever had her hair cut before.

But at the end, when she'd turned to face the mirror, she'd felt disappointed with the result. Instead of looking anything like as sleek and as chic as Ailsa in the French class, she looked like a curly-haired boy. In fact, she looked scarily like Finn – her older brother!

That was not what she had wanted. Not at all. She'd hoped that a short haircut would make her look older, more glamorous, and just a bit exotic and exciting. Not like a big, overgrown boy in hockey kit!

Several hot tears slid from Niffy's eyes now and slipped into her shorn hair. She told herself off for being so silly. Hair! It was just hair. It would grow back. It would grow just a little bit more every day and she would be fine. But one thing was for definite: she would never, ever cut her hair again. Ever.

Gina was also trying hard to fall asleep. Her eyes were closed, and although she felt very sorry for Amy, she couldn't help feeling relieved and proud of her mom and her stepdad, who were managing to make their business thrive, even when times were so tough.

Just as Gina started to relax and feel the very first touch of sleepiness take hold of her, a face swam in front of her mind's eye. Usually the person who she liked to think about last thing at night, with a secret smile, was Dermot. But now . . . She was startled. Her eyes opened wide. Why on earth was she thinking about Callum? What was Dermot's friend Callum doing in her mind last thing at night?

Min was the first person in the dorm to fall asleep. But no sooner had she let go of her real worries than she began to pitch fast-forward and headlong into her dream worries.

In her dream, Min was sitting in the St Jude's assembly hall. There were desks all around her and at every single desk was a St Jude's girl, bent over and writing furiously.

Min looked down at the pages on the desk in front of her and with horror realized they were completely blank. Totally empty. There were no questions. There were no answers. She was just staring at white sheets of paper.

Heart leaping, Min looked up in her dream at the big clock on the wall. There were just seconds to go. The exam was about to end! Why hadn't she said anything? Why hadn't she asked for another exam paper? What had she been thinking? Where had she been? Had she slept though this exam and just woken up?

Before the clock could strike the hour, Min woke up from the exam torture with a start.

For several minutes, she lay still, trying to gather her thoughts. It was OK, she told herself. She was still in bed in the boarding house. That was just a dream, even though it had felt so real; she could still see the clock, the blank sheets of paper and even the backs of the girls right in front of her.

A dream.

Just a dream.

She tried to calm herself, but her heart was still hammering. She had a horrible dry feeling in her throat, as if she had been breathing through her mouth. She sat upright in bed and listened to the sounds around her.

Everyone else seemed to be asleep. Amy was snoring slightly. Good, Min couldn't help thinking. She'd had a horrible evening and deserved a good night's rest.

After staring into the darkness for several minutes, Min decided that she would get up. Maybe if she went to the bathroom and drank a glass of water, she would get rid of this horrible, tense thumping in her chest.

The glass of water helped a little, but Min still wasn't ready to go back to bed. She didn't want to lie there in that dark dorm, listening to everyone else sleeping. She suspected that would make it even harder to drop off again.

Although it was against boarding house rules, she decided to tiptoe downstairs to the Upper Fifth sitting room. There she would read for a bit . . . maybe log on to her email . . . perhaps even make a cup of weak tea.

Min sneaked across the landing and opened the big fire door at the top of the stairs as slowly and as quietly as possible. The staircase was dimly lit with fire-escape lights and as Min began to make her way down it, every step seemed to creak.

Chapter Twelve

'Pass! Will you just pass?!' Amy urged Niffy as they ran side by side down the hockey field towards the opposition's goal.

Niffy was steering the ball expertly this way and that with her stick. She'd already managed to make it past two defenders, but Amy didn't trust her to get past a third on her own.

'Pass, you pig-headed glory-hunter!' Amy shouted in exasperation.

But Niffy was determined to get right to the goal mouth and to score this point herself. The match wasn't exactly going well. Niffy and Amy's team was down 3-1 to the team being captained by Penny Boswell-Hackett.

The rivalry between Penny and her friends and Niffy and Amy was always at its fiercest during hockey lessons.

Now, 3-1 down, Niffy was determined to at least equal the score before the end of the lesson. Penny, Niffy and Amy took even the matches played in hockey lessons very, very seriously. The scores were personal.

Just as Amy had predicted, the final defender before the goal snatched the ball from Niffy and walloped it up to the other end of the field.

Penny, who had been running down to tackle Niffy herself, couldn't resist sneering at Niffy with the words, 'Yeah, you may look like a boy, but you don't play like one.'

Then she ran off up the field, hoping to score a fourth goal.

Niffy stood still, knocked breathless with hurt.

No matter how many nice things her friends had said about her hair, this one insult had undone all their good work.

It had to be true.

She *did* look like a boy. Her lanky frame and broad shoulders, topped with this curly mop-head, was horribly boyish.

'Pay no attention!' Amy urged. 'That girl is just a total cow!'

Niffy put her hands up to her head to smooth

down the short curls. The haircut still felt so raw and strange. Even worse, it felt cold. The winter wind now whistled round her neck and got in around her ears and under her collar in a way it had never done before.

In bed last night, Niffy had gone through all the options, including: somehow finding the money to pay for hair extensions; wearing a hat at all times; even buying a wig. But she had come to the conclusion that she didn't want to attract any more attention. She was just going to have to grin and bear it until her hair grew back.

The fact that hair grew at a pitiful centimetre a month was something she wished that she didn't know.

'Foul!' Niffy heard someone further up the pitch call, so the games teacher blew her whistle and play stopped for a few moments. Enough time for Amy to come over again and slap Niffy playfully on the back.

'Look, it's not as if she's so flamin' gorgeous that the whole world falls at her feet,' she said, gesturing towards Penny. 'You know what you have to do, don't you?'

When Niffy shook her head, Amy said, 'Your joke-shop stash. Don't use it all on the Neb. Surely you've got something nice and juicy you can use on her?' Amy shot another glare in the direction of the B-H.

At this suggestion, Niffy's face brightened up again. 'Yeah! You're right . . . I'll take a good look through the selection. See what would suit best.'

'Gina! Phone!'

Gina was in the study room, half-way through the evening's revision when she heard the shout.

Phone calls at the boarding house were rare. There was only one pay phone, which was almost always occupied, and most parents, friends and boyfriends either emailed or called on mobiles during the hours the girls were allowed to use them.

Gina left her desk and hurried to the little cupboard under a flight of stairs where the pay phone was housed.

Picking up the receiver, she hoped this wasn't her mom calling back to say there had been some sort of problem. Maybe the big deal wasn't going to go through after all.

'Hi?' she said.

'Is that the lovely Miss Winklemann-Peterson?' asked a warm and teasing voice which Gina recognized immediately.

'Dermot!' she said with a giggle. 'How are you?'

'I have managed to tear myself away from my books long enough to give you a call,' he replied.

'Did it take you ages to get through?'

'No, first time lucky – all the good little St Jude's boarders must be swotting hard, not wasting their evenings chatting to terrible influences like me.'

'How's your revision going?' she asked.

'Terrible. Horrible. I see a row of Cs . . . even Ds . . . I might even fail history.'

'You will not,' she assured him. 'You're very smart and hard-working.'

'And good-looking?' he wheedled. 'Please tell me I'm good-looking too, otherwise I'm going to cry.'

'You're very, very good-looking,' she told him, but with another giggle.

'I've had an idea. I've thought of a way we just might be able to get together away from the clutches of the café.'

'A date?' Gina asked excitedly. 'Did you get a Saturday off? Can we go to the movies?'

'Ermmmm . . . well no, not exactly. Saturdays off are a bit tricky at the moment. But this Friday . . .'

'I can't go out on Fridays,' she reminded him.

'Well, what about if my mum comes and picks you

up and brings you to my house for a revision session? Do you think Mrs Knebworth might agree to that? Surely, even the dragon lady would find it hard to object to that?'

'A revision session?' Gina was disappointed. 'That doesn't exactly sound like fun.'

'We'll do some revision . . . but then we'll have some fun. I promise.'

'The movies?' she wheedled.

'I'm supposed to be saving all my money,' he protested.

'Dermot! I could pay.'

'No, no, definitely not. Come over, pleeeeeeeease. I'll get my mum to phone the prison warden.'

'Well . . . OK. But not hours of revision. Do you promise?'

'Promise.'

Although she had the receiver tightly pressed to her ear, Gina could still hear something very alarming suddenly coming from not far outside the phone booth.

It sounded like a long, piercing, blood-curdling scream.

'What was that?' Dermot asked, as he'd obviously heard it too.

'Dunno,' Gina replied. 'Think I'll go and find out.'

'Are you armed?'

'Don't be crazy!'

But she hurried out of the phone booth and joined the throng of girls who were rushing through the corridor towards the door of the Neb's sitting room.

'It came from in here,' one older girl said. 'Should we go in?'

She knocked on the closed door. 'Mrs Knebworth, are you OK?' she asked.

The hallway was filling up by the moment, girls coming down the stairs, along the corridors, piling out of the study room. Word was racing around that a hideous scream had just come from the Neb's private sitting room.

All at once the door flew open and Mrs Knebworth stood there, red-faced, with an expression of absolute fury across her face.

'Whose is *this*?' she demanded.

Her arm shot out and there, dangling from her hand, was a hideous-looking puppet. It was green and black with a tumble of hair. Its mouth was wide open and it had spiky-looking teeth which seemed ready to bite.

Its arms were held high above its head and there was

some sort of plastic contraption on them, as if it was designed to attach somewhere.

'Whose is this?' Mrs Knebworth repeated. 'Does anyone know? Is anyone prepared to own up?'

No one said a word.

'Someone attached this horrible thing to my very own personal and private loo,' she added. 'I lifted the lid and just about had a heart attack!'

Although these words were uttered in a deadly fierce tone of voice, a little ripple of giggles broke out at the idea of Mrs Knebworth being confronted by an evil toilet puppet.

'I will find out who put this there,' Mrs Knebworth said, her face set in a deep scowl, 'and I will punish the culprit. No doubt about it.'

She narrowed her eyes, directed another long, penetrating glare at the entire crowd in the hallway, then turned back into her sitting room and slammed the door shut behind her.

Gina looked around the electrified crowd and saw Niffy standing beside Amy. Some sort of look of understanding seemed to pass between them and Gina guessed immediately that Niffy was involved.

As Niffy turned from the hall into the corridor, other girls seemed to throng around her.

'Did you . . . ?'
'Do you know . . . ?'
'What was that . . . ?'
The questions were being asked in whispers.
'That is the JimLaBim Toilet Screamer 130,' Niffy answered quietly. 'That's all I'm saying.'

Chapter Thirteen

The minute hand was moving towards the hour on the big assembly room clock. Min stared up at the clock in horror. Any moment now and time would be up, the exam would be over. She looked down at her pages again and saw that they were blank.

Blank!! What was happening? What was going on? She picked up her pen . . . but there were no questions. She looked back up at the clock.

Her heart began to hammer in panic . . . then she opened her eyes and once again found herself awake in her dormitory, with a thudding heart, in the small hours of the morning.

She glanced over at her bedside alarm clock: 2.37 a.m. *Great.* She'd only had about three hours of sleep and she knew she would have to get up and have another wander around the boarding house before she could even think of getting back into bed again.

It was what had worked the other night. She'd gone downstairs to the Upper Fifth sitting room, drunk a mug of weak tea and flicked through some back issues of *New Scientist* magazine until she'd finally felt drowsy enough to come back to bed.

She would go downstairs and do that again. Anything was better than lying on her bed in the pitch darkness, worrying herself silly about the exams while she listened to everyone else sleeping contentedly.

Min tied her dressing gown in place and put her feet into her slippers. Then she began the creaky tiptoe down the boarding-house staircase.

Through the dimly lit corridors she travelled until she got to the sitting-room door. Only as she reached out for the handle and began to turn it did she realize that there was light coming from inside the room.

At first she thought maybe she should just turn around and hurry back to the dorm as quickly as she could. What if the Neb or Miss McKinnon were on the other side of this door? But she listened carefully. There was no sound, nothing at all coming from inside the room.

Maybe a light had been left on by mistake, Min wondered, and she began to push the door open as quietly as she could.

'Oh!' she gasped in surprise when she stepped into the room.

'Oh!' came the startled response. 'It's you! You nearly gave us heart attacks!'

Sitting on one of the sofas with mugs of tea in front of them were Zarah, another Upper Fifth boarder, and Clare from the year above.

'What are you doing in here?' Min asked in a whisper.

'Same as you, probably,' Clare replied. 'Can't sleep because you're stressed out about the exams?'

Min nodded.

'Same here.'

'Me too,' Zarah replied. 'But, Min, you're so clever, why on earth are you worried?'

Min gave a little shrug. 'I want to do really well,' she replied.

'But you will!' Zarah told her. 'You'll probably do better than anyone else in the whole year.'

Min smiled shyly at the compliment, but it still didn't put her busy mind at rest. 'I keep having a horrible exam dream,' she confided.

'Me too!' Clare told her. 'In my one, time is running out, there's hardly a second left and I'm scribbling and scribbling and scribbling but I know I've still got pages of stuff left to write.'

'In mine, time's running out too, but my pages are totally blank,' Min said, settling herself into an armchair opposite the two other girls. 'In fact, the sheet with the questions is blank too. And I'm just in a total panic. Even when I wake up, I still feel in a panic.'

'That's horrible,' Clare sympathized.

'What about you?' Min asked Zarah.

'I don't have bad dreams because I just can't fall asleep,' Zarah replied. 'I'm only sleeping about two or three hours a night and I don't have any dreams at all, maybe because my brain is too exhausted to even come up with them. And I'm covered in stress spots,' she added, lifting the hair at the side of her head to demonstrate.

'Me too,' Min admitted, showing off her own bumpy rash.

'You guys really need to see the school doctor,' Clare chipped in. 'She'll give you something for that.'

'Do you want some tea?' Zarah asked. 'We're drinking chamomile because it's supposed to make you sleepy.'

'Yes, but unfortunately it tastes of wee,' Clare said, holding up her mug and giving it a suspicious sniff.

'Is this the first night you've come downstairs?' Zarah asked, as she went over to the kettle.

'No, I came down on Sunday night and sat here for about forty minutes.'

'Oh, you must have just missed us,' Zarah said. 'We're usually here between about half two and half four in the morning. That seems to be the worst time.'

The kettle came to the boil quickly and Zarah took a mug from the wooden rack, stuffed a teabag into it and poured boiling water on top.

'So what do you do?' Min wondered as the mug of yellowy liquid was brought over to her. 'Do you read? Study?'

'A bit,' Zarah answered. 'Clare's helping me with my maths.'

'Zarah's helping me with my French,' Clare added with a grin. 'Did you know she's bilingual?'

'No,' Min replied as Zarah gave a modest shrug.

'My family's spent a lot of time over there,' she said. 'Min, is it true that your friend Niffy is the one who's playing the jokes on Mrs Knebworth?'

'Oh . . .' Min hesitated. She thought she was probably supposed to keep this information secret.

She gave Zarah a smile. Funny how they didn't know each other well, even though they were the only two Asian boarders in the year. Zarah looked very friendly, tucking her bobbed hair behind her ear and looking at Min with great interest.

'You do know something . . .' Zarah wheedled.

'Well, Niffy got gated because she was in one of the Lower Sixth dorms when a boy—'

'A boy came in?!' Zarah gasped.

'No. A boy was in the garden with this bagful of bottles—'

'Of drink?!' Zarah's eyes widened again.

'Yeah. And the Lower Sixths had a rope, they got the bag up and then the Neb caught them all, although they did manage to hide the bottles. And although Niffy was there, it was nothing to do with her and she's just really annoyed she's been punished.'

'So she's taking revenge?'

'Well . . .'

'You can tell me, I won't tell anyone, except Clare, who's listening anyway.'

'What else has Niffy got planned?' Zarah asked.

'I don't know . . . Hopefully nothing else, I think she's done enough.'

Wanting to change the subject, Min asked, 'Do you think it would be OK if I switched on the computer?'

'Yeah, sure, it won't make any more noise than anything else we're doing,' Clare replied.

Min took her mug of tea and went over to sit at the great big dinosaur of a computer in the corner of the room. She switched it on and waited patiently as it went through its long, whirring start-up process.

More out of habit than anything else, she clicked through to her email and watched as one lone item popped up in the inbox.

With a start, she saw that it was from Greg.

Not really wanting to . . . in fact, dreading the words she might find in this message, Min moved the cursor over and clicked the note open.

'*Min, I meant to ask . . . can we still email about our homework once in a while? G x*'

Min had to smile at this.

She emailed back: '*Of course, M x*'

'Were you emailing your boyfriend?' Zarah, who was now hovering behind her chair, asked next.

Min turned round with a start.

'Ummmmm . . .'

'You have got a boyfriend, haven't you? I heard about him from one of your friends.'

'Well . . . I don't know if he's exactly a boyfriend, I mean . . .' Min felt flustered.

'But you just emailed him?'

Zarah's eyes were fixed on Min with fascinated interest again.

'Can you tell me a bit about him?' she asked.

All of a sudden Min could think of nothing that she'd like to do better.

Chapter Fourteen

'Dad!!'

The following Friday, at exactly seven o'clock as promised, Amy's ridiculously young dad, Gary McCorquodale arrived at the boarding house to take her out for dinner.

Amy rushed into the hallway and threw her arms around him.

He hugged her hard and kissed her on the cheek.

For a moment or two, Amy didn't want to let go. It felt so safe and familiar to have the thick arms around her and inhale his 'going out' smell: soap, shaving foam and his favourite brand of aftershave. He smelled of all the hugs he'd ever given her from when she was little: '*Night-night, be good for your gran and I'll see you in the morning, princess.*'

Up until now, she'd always felt as if her dad was right there, strong and steady as a rock to look after her.

But now, for the very first time, he was admitting a weakness. He was telling her there might be a problem and the problem had the potential to change both of their lives.

Something about his hug was different: it wasn't one hundred per cent strong and reassuring; her dad was clinging to her as well. He was trying to get some support as well as to give it.

'Princess, how are you doing?' he asked her in his gravelly voice when they finally pulled away from each other.

'Great,' she said, and gave him her biggest, most cheerful smile. 'You look very smart,' she added.

Gary wasn't tall, or slim or even particularly handsome. He was a bit square and solid and his head was shaven. But still he had a presence. He looked strong and muscular and his clothes were sharp. The open-necked white shirt and the fitted black suit were top-notch, and his shoes were polished to a high shine.

Even his smell was unusual – not the typical aftershave you'd have smelled loads of times before, but something complicated which mingled black coffee with figs, smoke . . . maybe aniseed.

He took care of himself, he noticed the little details.

His nightclubs were much sleeker and more stylish than any others in the city.

Amy's dad was gay.

He'd not even admitted it to himself until last year. In a weird way, Amy thought she'd known way before he had. He'd not allowed himself to admit it, because he loved Amy more than anyone else in the world – although his mum came a close second – and he'd always thought a gay dad was one added complication in her life she probably didn't need.

'You. Look. *Smashin'!*' he told her with a wink.

Amy had gone to a lot of trouble. She loved to dress up anyway, but tonight she also wanted to cheer her dad up. She wanted him to feel that together they could take on the situation, take on the world. They weren't going to let this temporary disaster take them down.

So she was in a top of silky white studded all over with bright silver and gold sequins. Her sparkly silver shoes matched and made her feel princess-y. Her white jeans were long and tight and sported a designer tag. In her ears and around her neck were the very expensive diamonds her dad had bought her.

'Have you said hello to Mrs K?' she asked.

'Yeah, we're all set,' her dad replied, and held out his arm to his daughter in an old-school gesture of politeness.

She took hold of it and together they walked out of the boarding house and down the flight of stone stairs.

Parked in the driveway, gleaming in the lights from the window, was Amy's dad's car: a shiny silver Porsche. He clicked with his key, making the lights blink and the door locks pop open.

Amy felt a slight unease as she slid down into the leather-upholstered seat.

For how much longer would her dad be driving a Porsche?

He drove deftly through the streets until they came to the restaurant he'd picked for tonight. Together they went in to the dark and candle-lit space where waiters in traditional white shirts and black trousers hovered about the tables, brandishing huge menus.

'Fancy,' Amy told her dad with a wink.

'Oh, yeah,' he winked back.

'People will think I'm your girlfriend,' she teased.

'Not when they see how little wine I let you drink,' he pointed out.

But the mistake was made once in a while because Amy, when she dressed up, looked like a much older teen and her dad was only in his early thirties.

They were waiting for the first course to arrive when

her dad decided to stop the chatty small talk about school and her friends and how she was hoping to do in the exams and begin the much more serious conversation.

'So . . . obviously, Amy, I want to talk to you about the business and the difficulties we're facing,' he said, his gentle voice sounding calm.

He folded his hands together, placed them under his chin and looked at her.

'Yeah . . .' she said, feeling slightly breathless, sensing her throat close with a little choke.

'We're in a lot of trouble, princess. I might be able to keep one of the clubs . . . or I might not.'

'One!?' Amy heard the shrill surprise in her voice. 'But you own *eleven*!'

'I don't exactly own them, darling; I was running them with Bill and a lot of money borrowed from the bank,' came the reply. 'Bill has made an awful lot of money disappear and the banks aren't in any mood to lend me more. In fact, they want back pretty much everything I've borrowed so far.'

'So what are we going to do?' Amy asked, feeling her eyes well up and her voice wobble much more than she would have liked to.

'No panicking,' he told her, and patted her hand

reassuringly. 'In the first place, we'll have to cut our costs right down to the bone. Then I'm going to build my one club up again, make it the only place to be in town. Fingers crossed, I'll be allowed to buy a second very soon and then it all starts to rock and roll all over again.'

When she said nothing, just looked at him uncertainly, he reminded her: 'Princess, I had nothing when I started. I'm already in a much better position than when I started for the first time.'

Amy felt the wetness of a tear trickle down her face. 'But, Dad, we've got so many more costs now: the flat . . . your car . . . my school . . .' This last word came in a whisper.

He nodded.

'I'll leave St J's,' she said, trying to make her voice sound as firm and decisive as she could. 'That'll save us loads of money, straight away.'

Her dad smiled at her. 'It's great of you to offer. It's great of you to keep saying "us" and "we". You make me feel like we're in this together.'

He reached over, took hold of her hand and gave it a tight squeeze.

Just then, the waiter arrived and set down two very complicated-looking starters in front of them.

'This looks ... interesting,' her dad said, and shot her a little wink.

'If you didn't want to eat fancy, why did you choose here?' Amy asked.

'One last blow out,' her dad replied. 'It's gonna be beans on toast from now on. So, *bon appétit.*'

After they'd both tried a careful mouthful of the food, he added, 'The school is expensive. We both know that. But you're really happy there, you're doing so well and, to be honest, Amy, it's the last thing I want to give up. I'd rather sell the car and the flat first.'

Amy couldn't help giving a little gasp of horror at the thought of the flat going.

Home, when she wasn't at St Jude's, was a beautiful modern penthouse apartment on the riverside in the centre of Glasgow, with truly amazing views in every direction.

'*Sell* it?' she asked. 'Do you really think we'll have to sell it? What about if we rented it out? It's so lovely, surely someone would want to rent it? You could move somewhere smaller ... and I could even stay with Gran in the holidays ... you know,' – she tried to sound brave – 'if you didn't have room.'

It was horrible. Much as she loved her gran, living with her ... that was something from Amy's past. When her very young dad was out all the time, trying to make his business work, she'd had to live in her gran's funny little flat: three floors up with noisy neighbours and just a little balcony as outdoor space.

That was still where her gran lived, despite all Gary's offers to move her somewhere else.

'You can't leave your roots when you've put them down as far as I have,' was Gran's answer to the moving question.

Her dad was thinking.

'Rent out the flat? Sell the car? Cut our monthly budget to the bone. It might be enough, princess, it might just be enough. I'll need to go home and do my sums. You do want to stay at the school, don't you?'

Amy nodded, feeling too choked to speak.

'You won't be getting any pocket money for quite a while . . .' he added.

'That will be just fine, Dad, that will be absolutely fine. We'll pull through. What doesn't kill you makes you stronger, eh?'

The starter plates were cleared away, and minutes later the waiter returned with two enormous steaks, smothered in creamy sauce.

'Stick in till you stick oot,' her dad urged her with a grin. 'Who knows when we'll be eating in a place like this again. Best make the most of it. And Amy' – he suddenly looked serious – 'you won't let all this mess up your eating again, will you?'

'No.' Amy shook her head. 'No, I promise. You need me strong, Dad.'

'Yeah, exactly!' He smiled again.

Before Amy picked up her knife and fork again, however, there was something she definitely wanted to give her dad.

Ever since he'd picked her up, she'd been racking her brains for a really practical way in which she could help him and now she had thought of it.

Quickly, she undid the clasp of her diamond pendant, then she took the two diamond studs from her ears.

These had been big, extravagant gifts from her dad last year, when business was booming and when he'd been feeling maybe a little more carefree and flush than he should have been.

'Dad, I want you to sell these and put the money into the emergency account,' she said, holding the jewels out in the palm of her hand.

'Don't be daft!' he said, and closed her hand round the diamonds again.

'No,' she insisted. 'I really want to help. You're selling the car, so I'm selling these. Dad' – she looked at him firmly – 'you said we were in this together. So this is what I can do to help.'

Her dad looked right into his daughter's eyes and understood the determined look there at once.

'OK,' he said finally, 'if you're sure?'

She nodded.

'I bought them for you,' he said, making one last attempt to make her change her mind.

'I know and I love you for it, Dad,' she said quietly. 'Now you have them back because we both need the money more.'

As Amy finally started to eat her steak, she glanced around the dimly lit dining room, just to have a little peek at what the other diners were like and what they were eating.

Then she saw something so startling, she almost dropped her knife and fork.

No! It couldn't be! Really?!

'What is it?' her dad asked.

'Don't look now,' Amy hissed, 'but Mrs Knebworth has just sat down over at a table for two with her mystery Jaguar man!'

Chapter Fifteen

'Explain in your own opinion why the Jacobite rising of 1745 was unsuccessful?' Gina asked, then looked up with mischievous eyes at Dermot.

'Oh boy . . . OK . . . let me think. I know this . . .' He rubbed his face over with his hands, then began to recite reasons, ticking them off with his fingers. When he'd given the five he could think of, he looked at Gina for approval.

'That's very good,' she said, 'but you've forgotten about the food. The fact they didn't have enough food to get any further.'

'Ah!' Dermot smacked his head.

'Relax,' Gina said from where she sat cross-legged on the floor of the tiny bedroom Dermot shared with his brother. 'You've got two weeks till the Mocks and months till the real thing.'

'Relax?!' Dermot exclaimed. 'But I'm never going to remember all this stuff!'

'Shhhh! Didn't you remember five things out of six? C'mon.' She reached out her hand and touched his arm.

'Mmmmmm,' he said, raising his eyebrows, 'are we about to have a little study break?'

Gina's hand slid into his.

'Maybe,' she said, smiling at him.

He pulled her towards him and leaned back into the comfortable bottom bunk.

They began to kiss.

Dermot tasted of coffee and mint. His hair felt soft between her fingers and Gina kissed him enthusiastically.

He moved backwards onto the bed, pulling Gina along with him. They rolled over so they were side by side on the bed and the kissing continued, both pressing their lips together and using their tongues to feel their way around.

Dermot's hands were around her back, pulling her in closely towards him.

Gina opened her eyes and saw Dermot's closed eyelashes right in front of her. Something was just not quite right.

They were kissing, his arms were around her, but somehow, the tingle, the buzz, the magical little something hadn't started.

Gina closed her eyes again and concentrated on the kiss. No! This wasn't right. This felt about as exciting as chewing a piece of gum. What was going on?

Dermot broke off from the kiss and moved his face back so that he could smile at her. He looked happy and a little goofy. One hand under her chin, he pulled her face back towards his. Obviously it was all still working for him.

Gina ran her hand down his back and realized that his T-shirt had come untucked, leaving a little gap of skin above his waistband. She put her fingers on the smooth skin and felt Dermot flinch a little underneath her touch.

'Ticklish?' she asked, whispering the word against his ear.

'Very,' he whispered back.

'Do you think your mom will know we've stopped studying?'

'Yeah, she'll probably be coming to listen at the top of the stairs very soon, so if you want more snogging . . . keep going,' he whispered.

As they began to kiss again, Gina felt his hand move

to her shoulder and then – he put it right on top of one of her boobs and squeezed!

She was still kissing him and she didn't flinch or pull away. But still! She couldn't help feeling shocked.

That was her boob!

And his hand was right there, on top of it. It didn't feel particularly nice, this hand just sitting there, squeezing every so often.

Gina opened her eyes again to see that Dermot's were still closed.

She carried on with the kissing, not quite sure what else to do. Maybe she wasn't giving the hand a chance. Maybe if she left it there and let it squeeze a few more times . . . maybe she would get to like it. Dermot certainly seemed to be liking this a lot.

'Mmmmm . . . mmmm . . .' he mumbled whenever he stopped kissing her mouth and was in-between looking for a new place to kiss.

Just as he put his lips against her neck, there was a sharp tap at the bedroom door.

'I've brought you up some tea.'

It was Dermot's mum!

At the sound of her voice, Dermot rolled straight off the bed and onto the floor. He took up Gina's cross-legged position and snatched hold of a folder.

Gina scrambled to sit up on the bed and quickly smoothed over her hair.

Mrs O'Hagan was in the room before they were sure whether or not they'd managed the cover-up.

She had a tray with two mugs of tea in her hands.

'Hard at work, are we?' she asked.

She looked at Dermot closely. Now Gina could see that there was a little tuft of feather – one which could only have escaped from a pillow – nestling in his hair.

Chapter Sixteen

Niffy was bored. Bored, bored, bored, bored, bored. If she was any more bored, she would actually be a board.

Amy was out with her dad, Gina had been allowed to go over to Dermot's house for a couple of hours, Min was in the study and just about everyone else in the entire boarding house was glued to some TV programme Niffy could not stand.

So it was very lucky that she had a box still almost full of joke equipment hidden in a suitcase under her bed in the dorm. She'd moved the box from her locker one quiet evening when not many people were roaming the corridors.

Although the Toilet Screamer 130 was now in Mrs Knebworth's clutches and could never be used again, the blood-curdling yell had been very well worth it. Niffy still had hysterics whenever she thought about it . . . and she was quite enjoying the rumours going round the boarding house that she was behind the prank. Whenever anyone asked her directly, she would neither confirm nor deny it.

Raking though the box of jokes now, she saw many interesting things, but the one which really attracted her attention was a plastic tub full of bright green slime: '*Extra runny and quick-pouring.*' Excellent!

She lifted the lid of the slime pot and poked at the gooey contents, thought about it for a bit and then an idea came to her.

Stuffing the slime pot under her jumper, she headed for the boarding-house's main sitting room, where everyone coming back from their evening out had to sign in. Niffy had always wanted to know if that perching-things-on-the-top-of-a-door trick actually worked the way it always did in comics and cartoons.

Now, if she carefully propped the door open and then put the little tub of slime on top of the door . . . would the slime pot fall down and spill its contents all over the next person who walked in? Or what exactly would happen?

It was an experiment . . . For a moment, Niffy even considered asking Min along. Min loved experiments; maybe she'd like to monitor this one. But then, two people fiddling about with the sitting-room door might attract too much attention. Plus, Min never broke any rules and wouldn't want to risk getting into trouble.

Niffy headed down the corridors towards the room. She was careful not to glance at her reflection in the large hallway mirror, because it still gave her a fright.

Now that nearly a week had passed, it hadn't got any better with the hair. Sometimes, she almost quite liked it because it was so different, but most of the time she hated it and was willing her hair to grow faster. She'd even started eating an egg for breakfast every morning because eggs were supposed to be good for hair growth.

Now Niffy was at the door of the large sitting room where the signing-in sheets were kept. Because nearly everyone was in the TV room, the sitting room was deserted, save for a half-drunk mug of tea, which suggested that someone might be back soon.

Quickly, Niffy jammed the door slightly open with a folded section from the newspaper – the motoring section: she didn't think anyone in the boarding house would miss that – then she pulled a little footstool over so she could reach the top of the door.

Once she'd climbed up, she whipped the lid off the

pot of Slime and sat it nice and precariously in place on top of the door. She pushed it slightly to one side so that it had the best chance of falling directly on top of whoever was going to come in next.

Niffy could hear Miss McKinnon's voice outside in the hall. She was talking to someone and, after listening for a moment or two, Niffy decided it was Mel and one of her Lower Sixth friends.

Fizzing with anticipation now about who would walk in first, Niffy hid herself behind the sofa. If there was a big, gooey Slime Disaster, she hoped everyone involved would rush out of the room to clean up, giving her a chance to make an escape.

On the steps outside the front door, Amy was saying good night to her dad.

They gave each other a big hug and a kiss on each cheek. But even after the kisses, they didn't let each other go immediately.

'It's going to be OK,' her dad told Amy. He patted her soothingly on the back, just like he had when she had been little. 'It really will. It's only money,' he told her.

'Ha!' She tried to laugh a little at this, but trying to laugh only made her feel even more sad.

'I know you're going to rush off to work now, aren't you?' she asked him.

'Yeah.'

'But don't work too hard, will you? You'll take care of yourself for me, won't you?'

'I will take extra special care of myself just for you, princess.'

'Dad?'

'Yeah?'

'You won't ever . . .' Amy began.

'Call you that again? Well . . . no, not if you don't want me to.' He tried to put a cheery smile in place but it didn't quite come off.

'No!' She smacked his arm. 'You won't ever stop calling me that, will you? That's what I was going to ask.'

'OK, princess.' He grinned. 'You look after yourself too. Promise me?'

'Promise.'

He turned to go, but then stopped and looked at her with curiosity: 'You don't have a boyfriend right now, do you?'

'No!' she replied, surprised.

'No. I thought you would have told me if you did. But I'm kind of stunned – why don't you have a boyfriend? Why are you not fighting them off with a stick?'

'Ha, long story. Don't worry about it. I'm fine. Off you go, good night. Safe journey.'

She stayed on the steps to wave him off as he got into the sleek car and drove away into the night.

Only when the car had pulled out of the driveway did she allow her intense sadness at tonight's news to wash over her.

She and her very hard-working dad were going to have to move out of their beautiful home. They were going to have to let someone else move in and take over the huge black leather corner sofa and the jacuzzi and the roof terrace. Someone else would be looking at the views right over the Glasgow rooftops and out to the hills beyond the city.

And would that even be enough?

Would her dad manage to save the business? Would Amy still be able to go to St Jude's? She knew that she wanted to stay here at school, but she felt so guilty about the cost.

Her head was swirling with these frightening thoughts as she went in through the boarding-house front door.

She waved a quick hello to Mel, Rachel and Miss

McKinnon, standing in the hallway, and headed for the sitting room so that she could register that she was officially back.

As Amy pushed open the sitting-room door, a green plastic pot flew into the air. It bounced against the door, splattering Amy's face and her silky white sequinned top with a great cloud of green goo, then it landed on the carpet where the rest of its contents spilled out onto the floor.

This was too much for Amy; she burst into fierce and painful sobs.

'Oh, bum . . .' a familiar voice said from behind the sofa.

Then Niffy's shorn head popped up.

When Miss McKinnon hurried into the sitting room to find out why Amy was crying in there, she saw her slumped on the sofa, her pale top splattered with green, her face in her hands.

Hovering beside her was Niffy, who looked very concerned, but didn't seem to know what to do to comfort her friend.

'I'm sorry,' Niffy said, both to Amy and to Miss McKinnon. 'It was just supposed to be funny. A joke. I really didn't want to upset you. I wasn't even aiming at you. I didn't think you'd be back for ages.'

'What's that green stuff?' Miss McKinnon asked.

'Slime . . . extra runny . . .' Niffy admitted. 'If Amy would just let me, I could get it off her top and it's guaranteed non-staining.'

'GO AWAY!' Amy roared from behind her hands. 'Everything's just so ha-bloody-ha to you. Just a game, just a joke . . . does anything serious ever happen to you at all?'

With this, Amy looked up and both Niffy and Miss McKinnon saw her tear-soaked face.

'I'm sorry,' Niffy said again. 'And you know serious stuff does happen to me too,' she added sadly.

'Sorry,' Amy said, sounding a little calmer.

They were both thinking about Niffy's mum, who was fighting cancer, for goodness sake. Amy could have kicked herself for being so tactless.

Miss McKinnon spotted a tissue box on a side table and brought it over to Amy. Once Amy had blown her nose and wiped down her slime-splattered face, Miss McKinnon asked gently, 'How was your evening out with your dad?'

Unfortunately this made Amy burst into tears again.

'Oh, no!' Niffy understood a little better now. 'Are things really bad?'

'Oh dear.' Miss McKinnon sat down on the sofa

beside Amy, holding out the tissues. When she asked, 'Do you want to tell us a little about it?' she sounded so understandingly kind, that in between tears and tissues, Amy explained everything that her dad had said to her over dinner.

'But you're not going to leave St Jude's?' Niffy asked anxiously.

'No. That's not the plan. Not at the moment . . .' came the hesitant reply, 'but we'll have to move out of the flat . . . and it might have to be sold if . . .' Amy quickly pressed a tissue up to her face.

A girl entered the room, but at the glare she received from Niffy, she quickly backed out again.

'It's OK,' Miss McKinnon said, and patted Amy soothingly on the back. 'Things can work out in all sorts of unexpected ways. Your dad sounds really nice, really caring,' she added.

'Yeah,' Amy sniffed.

'It's good of him to tell you all this, even if it is hard to deal with. At least you know exactly what's going on. When my parents were having problems . . .' Miss McKinnon hesitated.

Amy and Niffy both looked at her expectantly, encouraging her to tell them more.

'Well, they tried to keep it to themselves,' Miss

McKinnon said, 'but then we would catch little whispers and rumours and we were sure something terrible was happening. I think it's much better if families can get things out in the open. Then you can all pull together.'

'There's only me, my dad and Gran,' Amy said. 'We've always been very close.'

'That's really nice,' Miss McKinnon said.

'I just wish there was some way I could help him,' Amy exclaimed. 'I don't want another penny of pocket money. I need to make some money and help him.'

'I'm sure he doesn't expect—' Miss McKinnon began.

But Niffy interrupted with the idea: 'eBay, Aim, you've got loads and loads of really nice things. You never wear even half of it. Why don't you have a sale on eBay?'

Amy seemed to brighten at this idea. 'Yes,' she said, looking round at Niffy with a slight smile. 'Yeah . . . there's plenty of stuff. Even here at school. Then when we pack up the flat, I can get more. That's a good idea. Unlike the blooming stupid slime, you nit-brain!'

'Are boarding-house girls allowed to have a Saturday or Sunday job?' Miss McKinnon wondered out loud. 'Because I used to work in a grocery shop one day a week from the age of fourteen.'

'Do you know?' Amy asked Niffy.

'I'm sure there was someone in the Upper Sixth who used to work behind a make-up counter . . .' Niffy said. 'I think she did it for the freebies.'

'And if you pick somewhere that also has a branch in Glasgow . . . ?' Miss McKinnon began.

'Then I can maybe transfer and do more hours during the holidays . . . what a fantastic idea! Maybe I can get a job in that designer shop: Cruise?' was Amy's next thought. 'Staff discount,' she pointed out.

'Errrrr . . . you're supposed to be making money,' Niffy reminded her, 'not finding new ways to spend it.'

'How did it work out for your family?' Amy turned back to Miss McKinnon. 'Did you turn the corner? Did everything work out OK in the end?'

'Well . . . my mum and dad's shop went bust. We lost the big flat above it . . . and for a while it did feel as if we were left with absolutely nothing.'

Amy's eyes widened.

'I know, it sounds terrible . . . and it was terrible for a bit. But that's when we moved to Barra. Mum and Dad ran the village shop for the owner, who was ill. They'd seen an ad in a newspaper. And we all loved Barra . . . all my family live there still. We own that shop and a café now. It's just me who wanted to spread my wings and have an adventure, so I came to Edinburgh.'

'Wow ... you lost everything and moved to an island,' Amy repeated. This wasn't exactly an enticing prospect to Amy. She was an urban girl who didn't like to ever be too far away from a place where she could buy lipgloss.

'So long as everyone stays healthy and positive, you can all cope with the money problems. The changes don't have to be bad.'

'I don't think I really want you to move to an island though, Amy,' Niffy said. 'How I am supposed to put a reasonable hockey team together without you?'

'Shut up!' Amy said. 'There's no way my dad can open a nightclub on an island . . . unless it's Ibiza, obviously.'

When Amy and Niffy had finished talking to Miss McKinnon, they walked down the corridor towards the stairs up to Iris dorm and that was when Niffy made her surprising announcement.

'I've been thinking about it a lot,' she began, 'and I've told Finn that if you and him still want to go out ... then you should. I'll get used to it.'

'What?!' Amy said, trying to keep the delighted grin from her face. 'Really?'

'There's only one condition . . .'

'Oh no . . . we have to keep it as an online-only romance?' Amy asked.

'No! You're not allowed to have one of those bad break-ups where you can never, ever speak to each other again. Because that would be really awkward.'

'Deal!'

Chapter Seventeen

On Sunday morning it was very quiet in the St Jude's study room. Almost every desk was occupied with girls busy studying for their exams.

The distant sound of the pay phone ringing was followed by a girl bursting in through the study door and calling out: 'Gina, phone for you!'

Gina got up with a look of surprise.

'Dermot's missing you,' Amy whispered to her.

'Must be,' Gina said, smiling. 'It's too early for California.'

She ran along the hallway to the pay phone and picked up the receiver with a cheerful: 'Hi!'

'Errrrrm . . .'

The sound of someone clearing their throat was followed by a male, deep-voiced, 'Hi, Gina? Is that you?'

'Yes . . . who is this?' Gina asked, suspecting it

was Dermot, but not quite certain enough to say his name.

'Hi, it's Dermot's friend, Callum. We met in the café. Remember?'

Callum! Callum?

'Hi . . . is everything OK with Dermot?' Gina asked, thinking he must be calling to tell her something.

'Everything's fine as far as I know . . .'

Now Gina felt a wave of strange nervousness pass over her.

'So how are you?' Callum asked, sounding relaxed and friendly, as if he phoned her every day of the week.

'Me? I'm great. I'm studying right now . . .' she replied, 'How about you?' she asked, sounding stiff and formal, just because she was so surprised.

Why was Callum calling her? And why did she feel so . . . so tingly and jumpy and electrified by it?

'Are you working hard?' Callum asked, totally at ease.

'Mmmm . . . kinda . . .' Gina answered. 'How about you?' she repeated, still thinking frantically: *Why is Callum calling me??*

'Neither of us is working as hard as Dermot though, are we?' Callum asked, and gave a little laugh.

'No, I guess not.'

'He is so busy . . .'

'I know.'

'It must make it hard to get to see him,' Callum ventured.

'Well, I guess . . . I saw him at home on Friday, but only because I promised to help him revise.'

'But you've no plans for today?' was Callum's next question.

'No . . . well . . .'

Gina felt her heart speed up slightly because she had a feeling she knew what he was going to say next.

'I just wondered if I could take you somewhere fun? You know, maybe the cinema or something . . . take your mind off the big bad Mock exams . . . at least for an hour or two?'

'Oh!'

'Or have you ever been out to South Queensferry?' Callum asked. 'It's right on the water – there's a brilliant view of the bridges, you'll have to bring your camera – and a place that does great fish and chips.'

'Oh . . .' Gina repeated. 'No, I've never been out there.'

'You'll love it! We could take the bus down . . .'

Gina knew she would have to say no because – what

would Dermot think? Plus, she wasn't allowed out on Sundays right now, except on school business.

Was Callum really phoning because he was interested in her? This wasn't because maybe he wanted to see Amy or Rosie again? But he hadn't mentioned them. He hadn't suggested they should come along with her.

'Callum . . . did Dermot give you my number?'

'No! I looked it up. I don't think Dermot will mind though. He's too busy. He's very, very busy . . .' He gave a little laugh. 'C'mon, we'll have fun. I promise you you'll have a very good time with me.'

'But I can't today, I'm going to watch my friend play in a hockey match.'

This was true and she was relieved to have the excuse.

'What about next weekend?' Callum asked immediately. 'Have you got any plans?'

'I'm going to be studying very hard.'

'Poor Gina . . . everyone needs a break now and then, you know. Why don't I give you my number, and if you change your mind, just call.'

Gina and Amy huddled together in the spectator stands to keep warm. Going to watch Niffy's Scottish squad hockey practise because it was the one way to get out of the boarding house on a Sunday afternoon during revision hell had seemed like a good idea at the time.

But now, Amy and Gina were so freezing cold that watching girls weave hockey balls around cones down on the pitch below, had lost even the slight allure it had held.

'Only another ten minutes,' Amy told Gina as she glanced at her watch, 'so enough about me and my dad's collapsing empire. Thank you for all your support . . . but now the Gina, Dermot and Callum love triangle. More details . . . more juicy details please!'

'Shut up!' Gina insisted. 'I've told you enough!'

'So did you tell him maybe one day . . . or did you give him the brutal "never"?'

'Well, you know, I didn't want to hurt his feelings,' Gina confessed.

'Or yours.' Amy nudged her friend. 'He's very cute. Cuter even than Dermot.'

'I know, but Dermot is so nice and Dermot is my boyfriend . . . and Dermot squeezed my boob!' Gina blurted out.

This made Amy burst out laughing. 'In a good way?'

'I'm sorry: *is* there a good way? I dunno. It was just

like . . . like having my boob kneaded like a lump of dough or something.'

Amy snorted. 'On top of your clothes . . . or under?' she had to ask.

'On top. Oh no . . . under? Is that going to be the next thing?' Gina screwed up her face.

'Depends,' Amy began. 'Depends on what you say. You are allowed to say something. You are allowed to tell him what you think. What with it being your body and everything . . .'

'Have you had your boobs kneaded?' Gina wanted to know.

'Yeah, I thought it was quite nice. Anything that feels nice is OK. Anything that feels uncomfortable, you need to say, Gina.'

'But it's uncomfortable to say . . .' Gina began.

'Fine, just let whoever do whatever because you're too polite to say anything.'

'But what do I say?'

'Whatever you want to. Say: "Ouch!" or "Could you be more tickly?" or "*Ooooooh, baby, I like it like this*,"' Amy added in a breathless voice.

'Shut up!' Gina slapped her arm.

'So, Callum or Dermot?' Amy asked. 'Who would you rather have squeezing at your boobs?'

Gina quickly said, 'Dermot, of course,' but a blush of embarrassment spread up over her face. 'No. Neither. It felt weird having him do that. And you know what? When we kissed, that didn't feel quite right either . . .'

'Uh oh . . . is the great romance on the rocks?'

'Amy!' Gina protested. 'Anyway, what about Finn?' she asked, sure that this would change the subject.

'Oh . . . well . . . I've emailed him to see if he wants to meet up the next time he's in Edinburgh . . . now that Niffy has . . .'

'Decided to let you guys get back together,' Gina finished the sentence.

'But I've not heard back.'

'Maybe he didn't get the email?'

'Well . . . we'll see.'

A whistle blast down on the pitch below signalled the end of the squad practice session.

'C'mon.' Amy stood up and gestured for Gina to follow. 'Let's go find Nif and catch the bus back.'

The bus stop close to the sports stadium was mobbed. Teenagers in all different versions of sports kit were waiting for buses to take them all over town. As well as hockey squad practice, football teams, rugby teams and badminton trials had been going on this afternoon.

In the dim twilight, Gina was the one who spotted Amy's very handsome ex-crush first.

She turned away quickly, hoping that Jason Hernandez hadn't spotted her, and hissed under her breath at Amy: 'Don't look over my shoulder, I've just seen Jason.'

But too late, the deep, confident voice was already breaking over them.

'Hey, St Jude's girls?' he asked. 'I've definitely seen you all somewhere before, haven't I?'

Gina, Amy and Niffy all turned to see Jason and a couple of his St Lennox's friends, including the horrible, pompous twit Charlie Fotheringham-whatsit, walking over towards them.

Jason, in a rugby shirt and tracksuit trousers, his dark hair ruffled with sweat, action and the cool wind, looked just as jaw-droppingly handsome as ever.

'Hi,' Gina said coolly. Amy had been crazy about Jason, but Jason had only ever been lukewarm about Amy, with the result that Amy's feelings had been deeply hurt. So there was no way any friend of Amy's was going to be pleased to see Jason.

'Jason, always a pleasure to bump in to you,' Amy said, hands on hips, as sarcastically as she could possibly manage, even though she looked slightly shaken by the sight of him.

'Always lovely to see you too, Amy,' Jason said, but his voice sounded warm – the flirt. This was the only way Jason operated, in full-on flirt mode at all times.

'Hello,' Charlie piped up. 'So who's the lucky guy you've got with you today?'

For a moment, Amy and Gina wondered what on earth he meant. What guy? Where?

But then, to their horror, they realized what he had thought, just as Niffy piped up with, 'No, it's me: Niffy. I've just had my hair cut.'

She shrugged and tried to be casual, but the wounded look on her face was obvious.

'Ha! Niffy! Of course, sorry . . . it's dark,' Charlie said. 'Hey, Yankee,' he directed at Gina, 'haven't seen you around for a while.'

'Much to my relief,' Gina snapped.

Jason now asked Amy, 'Didn't I see something about your dad's clubs in the papers?'

A look of astonishment passed across Amy's face.

'Losing lots of money, in administration . . . something like that?' Jason asked.

'No!' Amy said, a little too strongly. 'No, nothing to do with my dad.'

'The White Tiger Club? That's his, isn't it?' Jason persisted. 'The one that we went to together,' he added.

'Yeah, but someone must have made a mistake . . . everything is fine with my dad's business.'

Amy was flushing up frantically.

How on earth could this be public?

How on earth could someone like Jason know about this?

She felt as if she could just about cope with everything, so long as she could keep it to herself and her closest friends and pretend to everyone else that everything was OK. It hadn't occurred to her for a moment that it would be in the paper, be public . . . and people as distant as Jason would be able to find out.

'Oh, there's our bus!' she said, sticking out her hand just to make sure the bus stopped, although with a crowd this big at the bus stop, someone else was bound to be flagging it down.

Gina looked up at the bus and could see that it wasn't the right number. It was only heading partly in the right direction, but she and Niffy immediately understood that they had to get onto this bus to spare Amy any further questions.

'It's OK,' Gina soothed once she sat down on the bus seat next to Amy. 'Don't worry about him. He's a creep.

You got rid of him months ago. Who cares what he or his creepy friends think?'

'Yeah,' Niffy agreed, hauling her hockey bag onto the seat behind them.

'But . . .'

Amy was fighting the desire to cry. She didn't want Jason to make her cry. Not again. Not after all the wasted tears she'd shed for him in the past.

'I didn't want anyone to know!' she blurted out. 'I didn't think anyone else would know! I thought it could just be private, between me and my dad and my closest friends. How stupid of me! Of course people are going to find out. And people are going to laugh and gloat and . . .' She swallowed hard. She wasn't going to cry. She really was not going to cry.

'It's going to be fine,' Gina told her. 'Everyone goes through stuff . . . through really difficult stuff. Everyone does. We're all going to be here for you and we'll help you get through.'

'Thanks,' Amy said and she squeezed Gina's arm.

She felt Niffy's hand squeeze her shoulder reassuringly as well.

For a few moments, she looked out of the window. They were whizzing down Princes Street, past the row of bright shop windows.

'And what he said about you, Niffy!' Gina said.

Amy nodded, suddenly remembering the insult.

'Yeah, unbelievable!' Gina added.

'Oh, let's face it,' Niffy said gloomily, 'I do look like a boy.'

Amy suddenly reached up and pressed the stop button.

'Huh?' Gina asked. 'Aren't we going to the bottom of Prince's Street? We can change there.'

'No,' Amy said, standing up as the bus pulled to a stop. 'I've got a much better idea. If we get off here, we can all go in to that Superdrug and we can buy Niffy a home highlighting kit, some lipstick, some eye shadow and some nail varnish. You are never, ever going to be mistaken for a boy ever again, girl.'

'What??!!'

Chapter Eighteen

The St Jude's boarding house had a small, cramped bathroom up on the attic floor with an old-fashioned bath, toilet and sink. This Sunday evening, the little bathroom was packed.

Gina was squashed into one corner, Rosie was sitting in the empty bath because there was no other space, Min was watching proceedings with a troubled face from another corner and there, in centre stage, was Niffy, seated on a chair, a plastic cape around her shoulders. Amy, with plastic gloves on her hands, was fiddling with wet bits of Niffy's hair.

'OK, I'm just going to brush this on in little sections all over,' Amy explained. 'Just sort of randomly lighten up your hair here and there. I think it'll look really natural,' she added, sounding scarily like a real hairdresser.

She had a broad brush in her hand and she dipped it

into a dish of pungent white goo which Gina was holding out for her.

'Have you done this before?' Niffy asked nervously. 'I mean, do you know what you're doing?'

'Look,' Amy began, patting the goo into Niffy's hair with the brush, 'how often do you think Gina and I have had our highlights done at top salons?'

Niffy made no answer to this, so Amy said, 'Loads of times. Trust me, I've been watching hairdressers apply dye since I was thirteen years old.'

'Yeah, but watching is not the same as doing,' Niffy pointed out.

'I thought you wanted me to do this?'

'I thought you'd done it before! I didn't realize I was your guinea pig. You're just testing this out on me before you dare to put any of it onto your own precious head.'

Now this . . . this was sort of true.

Amy knew that expensive trips to expensive salons were no longer going to be part of the Amy McCorquodale maintenance routine. So yes, she was interested to know how the home-highlighting was going to work because if it was a success, well . . . then maybe she would consider allowing Gina to apply this stuff to her head.

'It's going on very smoothly,' Amy tried to reassure Niffy, but then she couldn't help giving a 'whoops!' as a little chunk of goo fell down through Niffy's hair and landed on her scalp.

'What was that?' Niffy asked nervously. 'I do not want to look like a badger.'

'Don't be silly!'

'How long do you have to leave it on for?' Min asked, picking up the box and scanning the instructions.

'Probably twenty minutes or so,' Rosie replied from the bathtub.

Suddenly they could hear the fire door pull open and a breathless voice called out, 'Gina? Are you up here? Please don't tell me I've run up all these stairs for nothing!'

Gina called out, 'In the bathroom. It's OK, you can open the door, we're having a party in here.'

The door was opened very slowly by a fourth former who obviously did not want to run the risk of catching some Californian hippie naked in the tub.

The girl was very surprised to see the room so packed. She wrinkled up her face at the overwhelming smell of hair dye.

'Ammonia,' Min pointed out. 'NH3 suspended in a water solution. It's almost as stinky as my spot lotion.'

'It's the phone,' the girl said once she'd found Gina's face in the crowd. 'There's a guy on the phone for you. I think he said his name was Callum.'

At this, the bathroom erupted into shrieks of laughter and cries of 'Wooo hooo.'

Gina was astonished. 'What! Again?'

More whoops followed.

'I'm really sorry,' Gina told the girl, 'but I think you'll have to tell him that I'm out. Would that be OK?'

'Go all the way back to the phone booth?' The fourth former groaned.

'Please?' Gina asked. 'It's just so awkward.'

'I'd go and do it, but I'm up to my eyeballs,' Amy said, waving her plastic gloves and sending spatters of bleach flying.

'Watch it,' Min warned, 'or we'll have little bleached spots all over our clothes.'

'Yikes!' Rosie said from the bath. 'No one said it was going to be so dangerous.'

The fourth former reluctantly turned on her heel. 'OK,' she said grudgingly, 'but you owe me, Gina Peterson.'

For the next five minutes or so, Amy dabbed away industriously as Gina was questioned and teased about Callum.

'I'm not interested in him . . . I think he's just trying to be friendly,' she kept telling the other, over-interested girls.

'OK, we're going to leave that to cook for twenty minutes while I do your make-up,' Amy instructed, unzipping her large toiletries bag.

'To cook! You're not making soup, you know.' Niffy's patience seemed to be at breaking point.

But Amy paid no attention and just bossed her friend with the words, 'OK, sit still, close your eyes and first of all I'm going to put on a bit of tinted moisturizer.'

As she dabbed at Niffy's face with a sponge, there was another knock on the bathroom door.

'Apparently hair dyeing is in progress,' came the voice they all recognized as Mel's.

'You can't come in,' Amy told her.

'What do you mean, I can't come in?' With this, Mel opened the door. 'If you're dyeing hair, then you need me. No one else in the entire boarding house has dyed their hair as often as I have.' She ran a hand over her head to make her point.

Mel's current look was a spiky bob with thick bleachblonde highlights and just the faintest trace of a pink streak at the front. The pink had sent the Neb into a frenzy and Mel had been washing it twice a day for several days now in an effort to tone it down.

Mel pushed her way into the crowded room and bent over to inspect Amy's handiwork.

'Hmmm, is that supposed to be highlights?' she asked, sounding unconvinced, 'You've put that on a bit thick. It might come up a bit blonder than expected.'

'Oh, shut up, Mel, it'll be fine,' Amy huffed as Niffy gave a little gasp of concern.

'Well, don't leave it on for the full development time,' Mel advised, 'then it won't be too over the top.'

'Let's get it off, right now,' Niffy decided. 'I've had enough of this.'

'But I've not done your lips yet . . . not even put on mascara,' Amy protested.

'Let's get the hair dye off, *now*! Before I turn into something even more horrible,' Niffy insisted.

'OK, OK,' Amy huffed.

Rosie pulled herself up out of the bathtub and Amy began to run the shower attachment so that she could rinse Niffy's hair.

'Have we got lots of lovely plans for Valentine's Day?' Mel asked as everyone rearranged themselves in the space so that Niffy could get to the edge of the bathtub.

Amy and Niffy groaned.

'Valentine's Day?' Niffy said. 'No, I definitely have no plans for Valentine's Day.'

'Me neither,' Amy added, running the water over Niffy's hair and massaging at the cropped mop with her gloved hands.

'Has Finn still not been in touch?' Niffy asked, sounding surprised.

'No. And don't you dare say anything to him about it,' Amy warned.

'Oh dear,' Mel sympathized, 'but Gina, you've got a boyfriend. You must have something special planned.'

'Not yet . . .' Gina began. 'We've both got a lot of work on.'

'Guess what I'm going to get for Bryan?'

Before anyone could answer, Mel told them: 'Brand-new black and red underwear, then I'm going to wrap myself up as his present.'

'Eeeek.' Gina was the first to answer.

As usual with Mel, this was way too much information.

'OK, I think that's all the stuff rinsed out. I think we're supposed to add the conditioner that comes in the box now,' Amy said.

'No, don't bother,' Niffy grumped. 'It'll be fine.'

'What about Mrs Knebworth though?' Rosie asked. 'The big question is: does *she* have something special planned for Valentine's?'

'Huh?' Mel asked.

'You mean you don't know?' Amy asked.

Every head turned in Mel's direction.

'About what?' Mel asked.

'About the man in the Neb's life,' Amy said.

'NO! Tell,' Mel instructed.

'I'm going to go and dry my hair,' Niffy said, making her way out of the bathroom.

Everyone else huddled around Mel to give her all the little titbits and scraps of information that they'd heard, or in Amy's case, seen for themselves.

'They've been on two dates,' Amy informed her, 'one being a very swanky dinner.'

'No!' Mel kept repeating, astonished that somehow she had managed to miss this tantalizing gossip.

There was a loud shout of 'AMY!' from the hall.

'That's Niffy,' Amy said, jumping up from her perch on the edge of the bath.

Mel pushed open the bathroom door and there in the hallway stood Niffy. Her face, beneath the carefully applied moisturizer, blusher and eye make-up, looked thunderingly furious.

Her short hair was standing on end. It was still mainly brown but now it was also dotted with great frizzy, orangey tufts. It looked . . . *terrible*. There was no other word for it.

Every mouth in the bathroom hung open with shock.

Chapter Nineteen

The bedside alarm told Min that it was 2:47 a.m. She sat up and looked around the darkened dorm. Everyone else was asleep, despite the fact that it had been a very eventful evening.

Niffy had freaked out about her hair, Amy had stormed off, Gina had promised that the application of an all-over brown dye would return everything to normal, then Niffy had pointed out that yes, that was all very well, but when were they going to be able to get brown hair dye between now and Monday morning? There wasn't going to be a chance until Friday afternoon at the earliest.

'All week I'll have to listen to people's stupid comments at school! And what about the Neb, what's she going to say?'

That question had been answered fairly quickly by the Neb turning up in the dorm to wish them good night and having a total hissy fit at the sight of Niffy's hair.

'Luella Nairn-Bassett, what on earth have you done to your hair now?' she had demanded. 'Wasn't it bad enough chopping it off in the first place? Now you have to go and paintball it *orange*? What on earth has got into you?'

That was so cruel that tears had actually formed in Niffy's eyes and she'd not been able to think of anything to say in her defence.

Gina was the one who'd jumped in with: 'Mrs Knebworth, it wasn't supposed to turn out like that. We'll get it all fixed up with some brown dye, just as soon as we can.'

'Good grief! Brown dye? I think you'll need a hairdresser to rescue that disaster, Luella,' the Neb had added.

But on Niffy's pocket money, a hairdresser was out of the question; everyone in the dorm knew that. Her eight-pounds trip to the barber's shop had left her with exactly £22 spending money for the rest of the term. And her friends knew not to offer her any money because she would never take it.

Min looked at the clock now. The seconds blinked past and the minutes changed from 47 to 48 to 49. She threw back the cover, deciding to head down to the sitting room to see if her new night-time friends Zarah and Clare were there.

She didn't wake up and go downstairs every night. But since she'd first bumped into them, there had been another two meetings in the small hours. It was sort of comforting to share the insomnia. Min was sure she'd be even more lonely and stressed out at night if she didn't meet Clare and Zarah in the sitting room every now and then. Plus, it was fun to talk about Greg with someone as endlessly interested as Zarah.

Zarah thought that Min must be the luckiest girl in the world to have a lovely, studious boyfriend like Greg. According to Zarah, Min should be meeting Greg every weekend, at least for a coffee and a chat, even if they were both studying round the clock.

'Go on!' Zarah encouraged. 'Otherwise, some other girl is going to notice him and steal him away. You wouldn't want that, would you?'

'I have to wait until the spots have completely gone, though,' Min had protested.

Tiptoeing along the corridor on the ground floor now, Min was pleased to see the light seeping out from under the door. They were there! Maybe one of them?

Maybe both of them, but someone was definitely in the sitting room and could keep her company.

With a smile on her face, she pushed open the door.

Clare and Zarah looked up, at first in surprise and then with smiles of greeting too.

'Hey, Min,' Clare spoke first, 'come to join the three a.m. study group?'

'There are these equations,' Min began. 'They're just going round and round my head and I'm not going to get any peace until I can think of how to answer them.'

'Bring 'em on,' Clare said with a smile.

'What are you up to?' Min said, directing the question at Zarah as she rummaged about the room for a piece of paper and a pencil.

'Just reading,' Zarah replied. 'I'm supposed to be reading Jane Austen, but I'm actually reading *Heat*.' She held up the magazine to demonstrate.

'Tut, tut,' Min said with a smile.

Then she wrote the equations down on the envelope she'd managed to find in the bin and passed them over to Clare.

After reading them through, Clare took a pencil and began to work on the first one with a furrowed brow and a long: 'Hmmmmmmmmm.'

Several minutes later she added, 'Min, you really

don't need to know these yet, they're Advanced Higher level.'

But she carried on trying to figure them out.

It was very quiet in the sitting room, just the sound of Clare's pencil scratching as Min watched and the occasional flick of a page from Zarah's magazine. It was not difficult to hear when somewhere on the ground floor of the boarding house someone opened and then closed a door.

'What was that?' Zarah said, sitting up straight and closing her magazine.

'A door,' Min replied. 'I definitely heard a door shut.'

'Down on the ground floor?' Clare asked.

All three were thinking exactly the same thing: Was this another school girl, wandering about at night? Or was it the Neb?

'Which direction?' Zarah began, but Min just hissed, 'Shhhhh.'

Now they all listened, straining their ears. It began softly at first, but then grew clearer and louder. Footsteps, slow but steady footsteps, were moving down the corridor towards the sitting room.

'Hit the lights,' Clare hissed. Min jumped up to the side light beside the piano and clicked the switch.

Now the three girls were in darkness listening to the

clump, clump, clump as it came down the corridor towards them.

'It's the Neb,' Zarah said in a terrified whisper. 'We're toast.'

'Hide,' Clare whispered, so quietly it was almost under her breath.

Min crouched down behind the arm of the sofa, Zarah moved behind a curtain and Clare got up from her armchair and shrank down behind it.

Clump, clump, clump . . . The footsteps kept on coming.

Min pulled herself into a tiny ball.

When the footsteps were right up outside the door, they paused. All three girls inside the sitting room held their breaths.

The door began to creak slowly open. Min scrunched her eyes shut, held her breath and did not move one single muscle.

There was silence. Whoever had opened the door was standing there, holding it open, peering into the dark room and trying to decide what to do next.

It was Niffy! Min told herself. Niffy in her hair trauma couldn't sleep and had decided to come downstairs. Niffy was standing at the door trying to decide whether to risk turning on the light or not.

Well, if it wasn't Niffy, it was bound to be someone else from the Upper Fifth. Who else would come into the Upper Fifth sitting room and be standing there anxiously wondering whether or not to switch on the light?

Min decided to risk opening her eyes, just to see if she could get a glimpse of anything useful.

Just then, Zarah, behind the curtain, let out a squeaky, stifled, but unmistakable sneeze.

The overhead light clicked on and Mrs Knebworth demanded in an icy voice, 'Just who is hiding in this room? You had better come out right this very instant and face the music.'

Chapter Twenty

For a moment, there was absolute silence in the room. No one moved a muscle. No one even blinked.

'Who is behind the curtain?' Mrs Knebworth boomed, her voice loud enough to wake the entire boarding house.

The curtain moved and Zarah shuffled forward, her head bowed guiltily.

'Zarah!' Mrs Knebworth exclaimed.

As soon as Min and Clare realized Zarah had been caught, they got up too, not wanting Zarah to feel the full force of a furious Mrs Knebworth all on her own.

'Clare and Asimina!' Mrs Knebworth added in an outraged voice. 'What on earth are you all doing in here?'

She came into the sitting room, closed the door behind her and to their surprise began a thorough search of the room.

'Is there anyone else in here?' she demanded, as she looked behind armchairs, behind the other curtains and in any other place she could think of. 'Has anyone else been in here?' came her second question.

'No,' the girls answered, looking at her in bewilderment.

'No *boys* then?' she asked. She had stopped hunting; obviously satisfied that no one else was stowed away in the room.

'No!' Clare said, almost laughing at the idea.

'Well, this isn't the first time I've come across a night-time gathering and more often than not *boys* are involved.'

She said the word 'boys' with the deepest disapproval: the way some people might say the word 'criminals'.

'So what are the three of you doing here, out of your beds at three thirty in the morning?' she barked, tying the belt of her quilted pink dressing gown around her.

She looked totally strange to the three girls, because although she was wearing her thick, round glasses, the Neb was devoid of the pale Estée Lauder foundation and bright-pink lipstick which she wore every single day, not to mention the tweed suit and sensible pumps. Plus, her hair was clipped into a neat row of foam rollers.

171

'We were doing a bit of homework . . .' Min began.

'Homework?' the Neb repeated, her eyebrows shooting up towards the curlers.

Min pointed to the page with Clare's scribbles, and to Zarah's Jane Austen book.

'Why are you gathered in the Upper Fifth sitting room at three thirty in the morning to do homework, may I ask?'

'We couldn't sleep,' Clare explained.

Mrs Knebworth picked up the page of work on the maths equations, studied them for a moment and said, 'No wonder.'

Then she did another surprising thing.

She walked over to the sofa, lowered herself slowly down into it, then with a sigh, she ordered the girls to: 'Sit down.'

'Are the three of you down here every night doing homework?' Mrs Knebworth asked, once they'd settled into nearby chairs. No one dared sit on the sofa beside her.

'No,' Min replied. 'Not every night.'

'We've met up a few times, by accident really,' Zarah added.

'We've got insomnia . . . I think it's the exams,' Clare explained.

'Oh dear.' Mrs Knebworth gave another sigh.

Maybe because she wasn't wearing her tweeds and her pussy-bow blouse or her fierce pink lipstick, Min couldn't help thinking that Mrs Knebworth looked a little less harsh tonight; a little softer almost, a tiny bit fuzzy, out of focus even.

'Insomnia . . . oh dear,' the Neb repeated. 'Well, I know all about that. OK, you put the kettle on, Zarah, and maybe we'll all have a cup of tea together. I see you've got chamomile on the go, that's good. Very soothing.'

The girls looked at each other. If Mrs Knebworth had suggested going out to a nightclub together instead of sitting down to a cup of tea, they might have been less surprised.

'Tea?' Zarah asked, just to make sure she'd heard that properly.

'Yes, we'll have a little chamomile tea. I'll tell you everything I know about insomnia, then we'll all head back to bed and try to get a bit more sleep before the day starts in earnest.'

Min and Zarah exchanged a glance.

Did this mean they weren't in trouble? *Really?!* It was too surprising. There was nothing the Neb liked more than telling people they were in trouble.

The kettle went on and Zarah set out mugs and teabags as Mrs Knebworth began to talk.

'I always used to sleep like a log. Very soundly. Enjoyed going to sleep, dreaming deeply and waking up refreshed in the morning. But when George was unwell . . . Do you know anything about George, girls?' she interrupted herself to ask.

'He was your husband,' Clare replied.

Everyone in the boarding house knew that Mrs Knebworth was a widow, but not many girls knew much more about the story than that.

'Yes,' Mrs Knebworth answered. 'For nineteen years. We have a daughter, she's at university now. But poor old George, he got cancer and he died.' She said this a little too matter-of-factly, as if she was trying to keep all the emotion of these words tightly under control.

'I'm very sorry,' Min said. 'Was he ill for a long time?'

'About a year, Asimina, which isn't such a long time. But it felt like it . . . oh my goodness, it felt like a very, very long time, especially as my days were all about twenty-two hours long.'

Zarah handed Mrs K the mug of tea. The house-mistress held it tightly in both hands as she talked on.

She told them a little about George's final months,

when she'd been rushing in and out of hospital with all the stress of trying to carry on as normally as possible for her daughter.

'I couldn't sleep. You'd have thought I'd have been exhausted, with all the worrying, all the rushing around every day, but when I finally lay down in bed, I just stared up at the ceiling and sleep would not come. Hours would pass, and if I finally drifted off, I would wake up only a little bit later and it would be impossible to drop off again.'

Min nodded her understanding at this.

'When George died, you'd have thought that maybe the sleep problem would have solved itself. The worst had happened – nothing more to worry about. But it got worse and worse. Finally, when I was so exhausted that I fell asleep at the wheel of the car one day and landed up in a ditch, I decided I had to get help.'

The girls were all listening to Mrs Knebworth with fascination now.

It was so strange to hear her speak about herself, and for her to be talking just like a normal person, instead of barking instructions and sharp disapprovals.

It occurred to Min that she had never given much thought to Mrs Knebworth's life, not really. She'd never thought about where the Neb went when she wasn't at the boarding house or what her life had been like before she came there. To be honest, Mrs Knebworth never seemed like a real person – more like a boarding-house fixture. Girls came and went, wallpaper changed, rooms were re-painted, but Mrs Knebworth stayed the same for ever.

'I found out that you have to just relax in bed. If you can't get to sleep, just rest and relax,' Mrs Knebworth said, 'and it's very important not to worry about the insomnia. Never look at the time when you're in bed awake. It never, ever helps. Pretend it's the time you want it to be: two minutes after midnight with the whole night ahead or six thirty-five in the morning, not long until you get up.

'Share your worries with your friends too, then they won't seem nearly so bad and are less likely to keep you awake at night. I bet Asimina here' – she turned to look at Min – 'is in a total fret about her exams and how she won't do well enough, when she's one of the cleverest girls in the year! Asimina, my dear, you are going to get a string of As, as long as you don't deprive your busy brain of the rest it needs.'

'Mrs Knebworth,' Clare said. 'Did we wake you up tonight? Or have you still got insomnia?'

'Oh . . . no . . . I sleep pretty well these days, when I'm

not being disturbed by *boys* in the back garden,' the Neb said with a strict look, just in case any of them was thinking of inviting boys to the back garden. 'It's just been a strange time. I'm delighted to have Miss McKinnon helping me out, but it's a lot of work, showing her the ropes . . . and then there's George's cousin . . .'

Mrs Knebworth paused.

Min, Zarah and Clare all leaned forward in their chairs, breathless with interest.

George's cousin? Surely this must be the Jaguar man. What was Mrs K about to tell them?

'We used to be very friendly with him . . .' she went on. 'Then after George died, his cousin went to work abroad. Now, years later, he's moved back to Scotland.

'He's looked me up, of course, and we've been out together for a meal a few times. It's lovely to see him again,' she added, 'but it's thrown up lots of old memories and not all of them happy . . .'

Chapter Twenty-one

'Just two days to go . . .' Gina stated the obvious at breakfast the following Saturday. 'First exams on Monday morning.'

'All leave is cancelled,' Amy reminded them, as if they were likely to forget. 'What are we going to do around here all weekend?' she groaned.

'Study?' Min suggested.

'What time does the post arrive on Saturdays?' Niffy asked, whacking the top off her boiled egg.

'About eleven, I think,' Amy replied. 'Expecting something? Postcard from Angus?'

Niffy just snorted at this.

'Not likely. Let's just say I've sent a certain someone something . . . and you'll want to see her face when she gets it.'

'Niffy, do you mean Mrs—?' Min began.

'Shhhhhh!' Niffy cut her off sharply.

'But wasn't the toilet monster enough?' Min asked in a whisper.

'Nearly,' Niffy admitted.

'She's going to catch you, plus . . . I don't think you're being very nice.'

'Nice?!' Niffy asked in astonishment. 'Why should I be nice to the Neb?'

'She's not that bad . . .' Min began, causing Niffy's eyes to widen further.

'And,' Min went on, 'I think she's a bit stressed at the moment.'

'Oh, a bit stressed. Right, fine, well I'll try and remember that the next time she gates me for something that wasn't even anything to do with me.'

'But you did hide the booze,' Min had to remind her.

After this, no one said anything else. The rest of breakfast was eaten in silence, then most of the boarders dutifully trudged off to the study room.

Just before eleven, Niffy whispered to Amy and Gina to come with her.

She didn't ask Min, who would just have disapproved anyway.

'I can't be bothered,' Amy whispered back with a roll

179

of her eyes. 'Take Gina, then the two of you can tell me all about it.'

'C'mon,' Niffy tried to convince Amy, 'it'll be worth it.'

'No,' Amy said. 'If my dad's going to have to live in a bedsit to send me here, I have to try and do well.'

Niffy shrugged. There was nothing she could say in reply to that.

Niffy and Gina left the study room and walked along the corridor towards the main entrance hall where the post came in every morning.

'The plan is that we'll make tea in the kitchenette until we hear the postman. Then we'll dash out and offer to sort through it,' Niffy explained. 'I just hope there are plenty of people about when the Neb gets her letter.'

Just as they arrived in the hallway, the postman was visible on the other side of the glass door.

'Bingo!' Niffy exclaimed.

Catching sight of Mrs Knebworth in the large sitting room, the housemistress chatting to Miss McKinnon and a set of parents who must have arrived this morning to see their daughter, Niffy called out:

'Mrs Knebworth, the post's here. Shall Gina and I sort it out for you?'

'Thank you, dear,' Mrs Knebworth replied in her especially-sweet-for-the-parents voice.

Niffy opened the front door and brought in the bundle of mail.

Pulling off the elastic bands, she set the stack of envelopes down on the side table behind the door, then she and Gina began to sort through them. There were many boring-looking brown envelopes for the boarding house, a handful of air mail envelopes for the foreign girls, bank statements, credit card bills, charity requests, the odd stiff envelope that maybe contained an invitation and then – yes! There it was!

Niffy held out a large, bright yellow envelope for Gina to take a look at.

It was addressed to Mrs Knebworth, but that wasn't what caught Gina's immediate attention. No, the first thing she read was the black lettering printed across the front of the envelope.

The words, all capitalized, read: 'URGENT: DEMENTIA TEST RESULTS.'

Gina's mouth opened with surprise. 'Did you send her this?' she asked in a whisper.

Niffy nodded proudly. 'I think I'll take it to her right now.'

She picked up all the boarding-house bills with one hand, held the yellow envelope in the other and headed for the sitting-room door.

'No!' Gina whispered, half wanting to stop her friend, but half, she had to admit, wanting to see what was going to happen next.

Niffy gave a little tap on the door to which Mrs Knebworth replied: 'Yes?'

'Just dropping off your mail,' Niffy said, and walked calmly into the room as Gina hung about in the doorway curiously.

The set of parents in the room couldn't help staring slightly at Niffy, who was an unusual-looking sight. Her jeans were totally faded and torn at the knee, her jumper was long and tomboyish and her very short hair was still a patchwork of brown and orange which stuck up in an odd and frizzy way.

So far, she'd refused all offers of help to re-dye her cropped mop back to brown. She was convinced that any further attempts to sort it out were just going to make it even worse.

Yes, there had been a bit of teasing at school, but

most girls felt so sorry for the obvious hair disaster that they hadn't said anything at all.

'Here we go,' Niffy said, handing over the brown pile of bills and envelopes to Mrs Knebworth. 'And there's also this,' she added, with a flourish of the yellow envelope.

'What on earth is that?' Mrs Knebworth said, holding the bright envelope right up in front of her face. As she read the words on the front, Miss McKinnon and the visiting parents were easily able to read the large lettering emblazoned on the back of the envelope: 'PRIVATE – MENTAL HEALTH TEST RESULTS.'

There was some throat clearing by the parents, and Miss McKinnon began to blush.

'Urgent? Dementia test results?' Mrs Knebworth was reading out loud from the front of the envelope.

For a moment there was a totally embarrassed silence in the room.

Then Mrs Knebworth fixed a slow and deliberate look on Niffy.

Niffy's mouth was twitching as if she was struggling to keep it under control. Her special wide-eyed innocent look was firmly in place though.

'Hmmmph!' Mrs Knebworth snorted. 'And I suppose

you know nothing at all about this envelope, young lady?' she asked.

Niffy couldn't help herself. Usually she could pull off a prank with a completely straight face, but the tension in the room was unbearable.

The parents looked horrified, Miss McKinnon seemed to be hoping that the floor would swallow her up – and Mrs Knebworth?

Mrs Knebworth looked like Mount Vesuvius about to erupt into one huge earth-shattering explosion, but because she had parents with her, she was going to have to hold back.

All this made Niffy's shoulders shake with effort and finally a great snorty giggle erupted from her nose.

Mrs Knebworth handed the offending yellow envelope back to her.

'You take this, young lady,' she said, utterly calm, utterly icy, 'and we'll have a little word later. Thank you.'

Chapter Twenty-two

Min watched the minute hand of the big clock in the assembly hall crawl towards the hour. In just moments, this exam would be over. She looked down at the papers in front of her and wondered if there was anything more she could do.

She'd approached her questions slowly, methodically and thoroughly. She'd found them all surprisingly easy and now she'd carefully checked through her entire paper several times. She couldn't find another single thing to do.

Just like in her dreams, she watched the clock, but she didn't feel any sense of panic at all. This was fine.

It was already Wednesday, and she'd managed to get through three whole days of exams without any trouble at all. She was growing much more confident that she was going to do just as well as

Mrs Knebworth and most of her teachers had told her she would.

'Time's up,' a voice rang out across the hall. 'Put your pens and pencils down. Please sit still while we gather up the papers.'

The sense of relief seemed to flood through the room. Girls leaned back in their chairs, and Niffy stretched out her long arms and yawned.

As soon as they had filed out of the hall, friends huddled together in little groups to compare notes on the exam. It was the last paper of the day, so a big catch-up was in order.

'I thought it was fine,' Min told Zarah with a little twinkle in her eye.

'Yeah, me too,' Zarah twinkled back.

'Easy-peasy,' Min whispered, not wanting the group of girls on her left to hear.

They were moaning bitterly about the last question:

'We've not even moved on to that section yet,' one was saying. 'That was so unfair giving us that!'

'Totally mean,' her friend agreed.

'So . . .' Amy bumped her arm against Gina's. 'Did you survive?'

'Yeah, I thought it was OK and you know maths is not exactly my fave.'

'I know, me neither, but it was OK. So, are we going out for our one hour of special permission?' Amy asked, trying to keep the excited look from her face.

'Yeah! Min, you're going to come, aren't you? You have to buy a Valentine's card for Greg!'

Min looked embarrassed at the thought. 'Well . . . I'll come along with you but I don't know if I'll be sending—'

'Min!' Gina protested. 'You have to!'

Zarah also dug Min in the ribs.

This was Wednesday, and the coming Saturday was the fourteenth of February. So, after much arm-twisting, the sixth formers had persuaded Mrs Knebworth that boarders had to be allowed out this Wednesday afternoon. Just for an hour. They would all be back well in time for supper, but they had to be let out to buy the essential Valentine's cards, presents and all-important stamps so that everything would arrive in time for Saturday.

Valentine's Day – in a building with ninety-two teenage girls in residence – was a Big Deal. A very, very Big Deal. The postman had already joked that he would need an extra trolley bag for delivery on Saturday.

The only boarder who was not going to be going anywhere, for some time to come, was Niffy.

'Shall we buy one for you to send?' Amy asked Niffy as her friend strode out of the exam hall.

Niffy just snorted in reply to this.

'What do you have to do this afternoon?' Gina asked.

'I don't know yet . . . I'll probably be washing the Neb's underpants or something.'

A couple of day girls who heard this turned to face Niffy with their faces screwed up.

'Only joking,' Niffy assured them. 'Just.'

After the dementia envelope, Mrs Knebworth had decided that gating Niffy wasn't punishment enough, so Niffy was now doing chores in the boarding house to atone for her sins. She had already had to wash several floors, clean many windows, and she'd had to vacuum the tops of the wardrobes in the entire building. Basically Niffy was doing every unpleasant household chore Mrs K could devise.

Not far from St Jude's, there was a bustling little high street which had a smart stationery shop. This was where many of the boarders now headed.

The front of the shop was a riot of tasteful Valentine's

exuberance: red hearts, pink hearts, purple hearts, silver and glittery hearts and paper roses.

Inside, the little shop was mobbed with girls in green St Jude's blazers. But Amy, Gina, Min and their friends managed to squeeze in and join the crowds at the card racks. Just like everyone else, they began to rifle through the selection on offer.

'You *are* going to send one to Greg?' Amy asked Min.

Min, who was examining a card with a cartoon of a scientist on the front, considered the question carefully.

'Maybe,' she said with a little smile.

'You should,' Amy encouraged her. 'You two are stupidly letting exams get in the way of your lurrrrrve,' she teased.

'Shhhh!' Min said, looking embarrassed, but she didn't put the card down.

'What about you?' Gina asked Amy.

'What about me?' Amy was also holding a card, which she continued looking at so that Gina couldn't see the expression on her face.

'Well, you were all keen to come down here and everything . . . Who are you planning to send a card to?'

189

'My dad,' Amy replied, but there was just something a little jokey about this. Gina didn't quite believe it.

'Well, that's very nice and very thoughtful, but don't you think Finn deserves something? Just a little message to show you're still thinking of him?'

'He knows I'm still thinking of him. I've emailed him twice now. No reply! And will he send me something?' Amy asked. 'That's the problem. I don't want him to know that I'm thinking of him, if he's not going to send something back.'

'But he won't know the card is from you,' Gina pointed out. 'You don't sign it, you keep him guessing, that's the whole point!'

'Hmmmmm . . .' was all Amy said. Now she was holding the card against her chest. Gina couldn't see it, so couldn't tell if it was the kind of card you'd send to your dad or to the cute guy you were still very interested in.

'You're going home at the weekend, aren't you?' Gina asked Amy.

Amy nodded. 'It'll only be "home" for a few more days. I've got to help Dad pack up.'

There was a pause. Amy didn't want to say any more and Gina understood not to ask any further.

'Not *still* trying to get Niffy's brother to like you?'

Amy, Gina and Min looked up in surprise at the sneering voice which had shot this comment over from the other side of the card rack.

There was Penny B-H, pulling a face at them.

What was her problem? She could just never, ever leave Amy alone. Always had to prove how superior she was by teasing her at every possible opportunity.

'Why don't you just mind your own business,' Amy replied calmly.

'Huh!' was all Penny said. Then she turned on her heel and went over to the counter to pay.

'Who's she buying a card for?' Gina whispered to Amy. 'I thought she and that Llewellyn guy broke up ages ago?'

'Who knows and who cares,' was all Amy said with a shrug.

'Hey, Amy,' Gina said in a whisper, not wanting Min to hear, 'do you think we should send Min and Niffy an anonymous card each? And what about Mrs Knebworth?'

'Min and Niffy, no,' Amy replied. 'Way too obvious. They'll know. And Mrs Knebworth?! Have you gone stark, staring mad?'

'It'll be fun,' Gina said. 'She's been seeing this guy; she's giving Niffy such a hard time. Why don't we just send her a card to mess with her mind?'

'Card? No . . .' Amy said. 'I've just had a much better idea.'

Chapter Twenty-three

On Friday evening, at 4.50 p.m. exactly, Min sat down at the Upper Fifth sitting-room terminal and logged on to chat to her two exam correspondents, just as she'd done every day of the exams so far.

She opened up her email and saw that the message from her mum was already in the inbox, asking her how today had gone.

'*Really well,*' she typed. '*French wasn't so bad . . . Biology fine and maths quite easy, I think! How's your day going?*'

'*Fine,*' her mum, who had been waiting in her cramped office for this e-conversation, typed back.

'*How's everyone at home?*' Min asked next.

'*Everyone's great. They send their love. We're all missing you, as usual, big girl. It seems a long time to wait until you are home again.*'

'*I know,*' Min typed back and felt just a little achy at the words.

'*But the time will pass quickly if you study hard. We love you, Asimina. Try and have some fun when the exams are over. I've put a little extra pocket money in your account. Have a little treat. What about that nice boy you talked about? Why don't you take him to the pictures?*'

'*Maybe! Thank you, love you, Mum . . . going to go now. Byeeeeeee xxxxx*'

'*Bye bye, A xxx*'

Min didn't have too much time to think about the rest of her family and how they were doing because it was now 4.55 p.m. Time for her next e-speak.

'*Hi!!!*' she typed. '*Are you there?*'

'*Yes. How did it go today?*' came the immediate response from Greg.

'*Pretty good, I think. How about you?*'

'*Maths was horrible. Everything else fine.*'

'*Really? I thought our maths paper was easy.*'

'*That's because you = genius.*'

'*Funny. Ha-ha.*'

'*You taking some time off studying at the weekend?*'

'*Yeah. Think I need a break. My brain's cooking.*'

Min paused, she didn't hit Send yet. Hadn't he just asked her what she was doing at the weekend?

Min could feel butterflies leap up in her stomach. There weren't any more exams . . . Did she want to go out with her friends? Or with Greg? Maybe she could meet him with her friends? Maybe then it wouldn't be so scary. They hadn't seen each other since before Christmas. It was bound to be nerve-racking.

OK, but what had Zarah said? Meet up with him, before someone else snatches him away. Min definitely didn't want that to happen. Good grief! Even her mum was telling her to take him out!

It was time for super-swot girl Min to do something really exciting and rebellious . . .

'*Would you like to do something on Saturday?*' she typed. Crossing her fingers, holding her breath, she hit Send.

There seemed to be too long a pause before his reply dropped. Then there it was:

'*Saturday is Valentine's Day . . . did you realize?*'

Min felt her face fall.

'*Oh well . . . if you have other plans, don't worry . . .*' she typed back, feeling as if something had withered and died inside. Someone else had come and snatched him away.

'No! No, I mean it's Valentine's . . . we could go and do something nice like . . . eat heart-shaped cakes at that café you took me to???!!'

'Oh! Yes . . . I think that sounds very nice. I haven't seen you for ages.'

'I know . . . will we recognize each other?!'

'Yes! Is seven o'clock good for you? At the Arts Café?'

'It's a date,' he replied.

'Oh, really!'

Just then Amy poked her head round the sitting-room door.

'Bye, Min,' she called across. 'I'm off to Glasgow. Have a great weekend and I hope you get loads of Valentines! Or maybe just one important one!'

'Bye, Amy.' Min looked up. 'I'm going to meet Greg on Saturday night at the Arts Café!' she said excitedly.

'YES!'

'But won't all the cafés be full of tables of twosomes and roses and all that stuff?'

'YES!' Amy replied. 'That's the point! Finally, you two can tell each other how much you care!'

Min couldn't help smiling at the thought of Greg and a cosy table for two. But . . . 'oh no, you won't be here to help me do my make-up,' she said, looking anxious. 'The spots are better, but I could still do with a little touch.'

'No worries, I'm sure you look one hundred per cent pure dead delicious to Greg,' Amy assured her. 'Where's Nif, anyhow?'

'Niffy said she had one of her chores in the laundry room,' Min replied.

'Ta.'

With that Amy closed the sitting-room door and went over to the boarding-house laundry room. This was one of the most old-fashioned rooms in the whole place.

It had a stone floor, great big worn porcelain sinks on fat white porcelain legs and two industrial-sized washing machines. Probably girls had been doing laundry in this room ever since this house had been built back in the 1800s.

Crouched down underneath the sinks was Niffy.

'I'm heading to Glasgow,' Amy announced as she came into the room.

'Oh, yeah.' Niffy turned round. 'Hope it goes OK.'

'What on earth are you doing?'

Niffy, in long pink rubber gloves, was holding a knitting needle and poking at the underneath of the sink.

'Cleaning out the plug holes,' she answered as a long trail of mushy, stringy grey goo emerged on the end of her needle. She plopped it unceremoniously into the plastic basin she had at the ready.

'Oh, that is disgusting,' Amy said, stepping a little closer and pulling a face. 'What is that?'

'Soap scum and dirt mixed up with lots and lots of hair,' came the gloomy reply. 'All this long hair. It's everywhere.'

Amy looked a little nauseous now. 'That is disgusting,' she repeated.

'Yeah, the Neb's worst job so far. I'll probably have to lick the toilets clean next.'

'Stop it!' Amy squawked.

'Yeah . . . what was Min saying about the Neb not being too bad? Well, she should come in here and see what I'm doing.'

'You should have taken Min's advice and not played that last trick then,' Amy said. 'You're the one poking goo out of a sink drain. Min's in the sitting room arranging her Valentine's date.'

'Huh.'

'I've got to go,' Amy said, checking her watch, 'but those rubber gloves are going to come in handy for that job we talked about.'

*

'You get it out. I don't want to touch it. The paper's gone all soggy.' Gina pulled a face. 'Gross!'

Niffy, holding the lid of the toilet cistern in her hands, looked down into the water. The bottle of wine had been hidden in there for several weeks now and the paper labels were flapping off. Still, Niffy put her rubber-gloved hand into the water and brought the bottle out. It dripped all over the toilet and the cubicle floor.

'Towel?' she suggested.

Gina darted out of the cubicle. When she came back, she reluctantly handed over one of her own towels which she'd taken from its peg in the bathroom.

Niffy wrapped the bottle up in the towel and tucked it under her arm to carry it back to their dorm.

Two of the bottles – one of wine and one of cider – had already been returned to the Daffodil dorm and Milly, in a fit of generosity, had told Niffy that she and Gina could keep the third as a thank-you present.

But Amy had suggested that the bottle of wine, labelled with a mysterious note, should be Mrs Knebworth's Valentine's surprise.

'She won't think that one of us would have gone to the effort of buying her wine,' Amy had explained, 'so she's bound to think it's something to do with her mystery man. Trust me, this will be much more convincing than just some anonymous card.'

Back in the dorm, Gina and Niffy unwrapped the bottle. Most of its paper label came off as they took away the towel.

Now it was just a plain bottle of red wine with a plastic top.

'It doesn't look very impressive,' Gina said.

'Yeah, but by the time we've finished with it . . .' Niffy turned to the label and ribbon that Amy had left out for them.

'The bottle looks naked.'

But Niffy was already writing on the label.

'Don't make it too fancy,' Gina reminded her. 'Amy said if it's supposed to be a present from a man, it's got to be very plain.'

'How's this?' Niffy held the label up. It said: '*I could be yours. Drink me, Norah K.*'

Gina burst out laughing.

'Norah! I still can't believe that's her name!'

Niffy tied the brown label onto the bottle with the string, then made an attempt at a bow.

Gina applauded. 'That is perfect. That definitely looks like a guy present.'

Niffy seemed to wince at this.

'I don't mean you're like a guy,' Gina added quickly. 'Niffy, of course you're not like a guy. You know that. You just have a kinda practical way of doing things. Not girlie.'

Niffy was still scowling.

'Loads of famous, beautiful and elegant women aren't girlie,' Gina went on.

'Yeah?' Niffy didn't look convinced. 'Like who?'

'Like . . . Katherine Hepburn, Hilary Swank, Cate Blanchett . . .'

'It's not my fault that I'm built like a boy.' Niffy pulled her school cardigan down to demonstrate how flat her chest was.

'It doesn't matter. All models have flat chests and anyway, boobs are over-rated. Boys sometimes forget all about you and can only think about your boobs.'

This at least made Niffy giggle.

'Talking of boys and boobs . . .' she asked innocently. 'What are you and Dermot doing on Valentine's?'

'Did Amy tell you about the boob thing?!'

'Maybe . . .'

'Did you tell anyone else?'

'Maybe . . .'

'You shouldn't have!'

'I know . . . but what *are* you doing on Saturday?'

'Dermot has to work in the café. It's staying open late . . . for all the couples who want to go out together but don't want to commit to dinner, apparently.'

'So we're all going to the café then?'

'Yeah . . . I guess . . . probably Mrs Knebworth's going to have a more exciting Valentine's Night than us.' Gina groaned. Then she thought of something else.

'Did you send Angus a card?' she asked Niffy.

'Ha!' Niffy replied. 'I don't think he deserves one.'

Chapter Twenty-four

It was early Saturday morning, and Amy was kneeling in front of her huge white wardrobe with its six doors. On the bed behind her was a collection of cardboard boxes. She was supposed to be sorting out all the clothes, shoes, handbags and who-knew-what-else she would find in there.

Some of the boxes would go to her gran's home, some would go with her dad, and one box would come back to school with her. But most of the boxes were supposed to be full of things to sell. She'd written 'eBay' in big black letters on the sides.

But now . . . now that she looked at the racks and racks in front of her, it just seemed too big a job.

She had to get on with it though, because once she'd finished in here, she was supposed to help her dad sort through the rest of the flat and pack up everything else.

She could hear him moving about out there, pushing boxes around.

'How are you getting on?' he called out.

'Fine,' she answered straight away, even though it was a big fat lie.

She stood up and pulled a handful of clothes down from the clothes' rail, tossing them onto the bed. She turned back to the wardrobe and there, hanging right in front of her, was the astonishing white dress which she'd worn to the summer ball last year: an amazing creation of satin, chiffon and silky soft white feathers. It had come from Harvey Nichols, at a breathtakingly high price. Over a thousand pounds, she remembered with a wince.

There weren't going to be any Harvey Nichols spending sprees for some time now.

She brought the dress out of the wardrobe and held it up against herself.

Should she sell it? Should she keep it?

Would she ever wear it again?

Would she ever again feel proud and confident enough to go out in this?

Thoughts of last summer's ball flooded over her . . . how amazing she really had looked, of how Jason, her crush of all crushes, had just about *begged* to kiss her.

Amy held the dress in front of herself, looked hard in the mirror and didn't know if she would ever again feel as good as she had done on that summer night.

Jason had been hopeless, she'd broken up with Finn – by the looks of it, for good – and now this horrible stuff was going on with her dad. They were moving out of their home and tenants were moving in. She didn't honestly know when or if she'd ever be living here again.

She felt a small tear of pain and confusion slip down her face.

There was a tap at the door, so she quickly put the feather dress down on the bed, wiped her hand over her cheeks and set a smile in place.

Her dad had enough worries on his mind. She didn't want to add to his troubles.

He opened the door, holding a mug of tea in his hand.

'Drink of heroes,' he said, coming into the room and handing it over to her.

'Don't mind if I do,' she added, shooting him a wink.

He sat down on the bed beside the dress. 'Wow,' he said, stroking the feathers. 'I'd forgotten about this number.'

'It was very expensive.'

'Yes, I remember that!'

'I'm sure I'll be able to get a good price for it.'

'What d'you mean?'

'I'm going to sell loads of my old stuff – my really fancy, designer stuff – and hopefully make some money. I don't want you to worry about me, Dad, I'm going to try and pay my own way . . . a bit. I'm going to get a weekend job as well.'

Her dad put his arm around her and hugged her tight.

'That's my girl,' he told her, 'but don't worry. This is temporary. It's only money: it comes in, it goes out. It'll come in again. I'll make sure of that. Don't sell the dress,' he said. 'You've got to hang on to the good times. And doesn't every girl have to have something fantastic hanging in the wardrobe at the ready?'

Amy rested her head on her dad's shoulder.

'Hey.' He pulled something from the pocket of his dressing gown. 'Happy Valentine's Day,' he said, and handed her a shiny, foil-wrapped chocolate heart.

'Oh! Thanks.'

Her eyes felt all blurry again. This was probably going to be her one and only Valentine.

'Well, we'd better get on with the job.'

'Yeah,' she agreed. But as soon as he went out of the room, she stared at the rows and rows of clothes and shoes ahead of her and wondered how on earth she would manage to do this on her own.

'There's a van pulling up in the driveway . . . the man's coming out with bunches of flowers!'

Every St Jude's boarder who'd heard Tricia from the Upper Sixth call this out suddenly found a reason either to get to a window, or to make their way to the entrance hall, just for a little look . . . not that anyone was hoping for, let alone *expecting* flowers . . .

As the delivery man came in with three big bouquets and two baskets of blooms in his arms, there was an audible gasp.

Everyone looking at the flowers wanted to be one of the girls who was going to get them. *Flowers!* Bunches of flowers on Valentine's Day! That was just too romantic for words.

Mrs Knebworth scuttled out of her sitting room to inspect the delivery man's offerings.

'Oh my goodness!' she said. 'Let me help you with those.'

Really she was just as eager as everyone else to see who the bouquets and baskets were addressed to.

Gina, Niffy and Min were all milling about in the corridor leading to the entrance hall, along with lots of other girls – everyone just about ready to burst with curiosity.

'Right,' Mrs Knebworth said, laying the bouquets down on a side table, 'shall we find out who the lucky girls are?'

For a few moments, there was rustling as she looked for name cards on the bouquets.

'Florence Goldie,' she called out, 'in the Upper Sixth. Does anyone know where she is?'

The name was called out down the corridor and someone took off in the direction of Florence's dorm.

'Then there's Celia Walker and Jenny McCallan.'

Again the names were shouted out around the boarding house.

Gina, Min and Niffy glanced at each other. There was something just a little bit hopeful in Gina's face. Maybe Dermot would surprise her? Maybe he'd sent that cute little basket on the table there, overflowing with pink roses.

Min and Niffy looked giggly – neither was expecting anything – but as Celia walked red-faced along the corridor to pick up her flowers, Niffy couldn't resist a whistle and a little: 'Ooooh, lucky you!'

'Rosie Clayton,' Mrs Knebworth said next, making Niffy and Gina giggle. Amy's younger friend Rosie was going to be teased to bits for this.

'It's from my mum . . . definitely from my mum!' Rosie insisted as she made her way down the corridor to collect the first little basket of flowers.

'And . . . last but not least,' Mrs Knebworth said, holding up the little basket of roses and enjoying the fact that so many eyes were turned on her expectantly.

'The label says: *The Nifster Nairn-Bassett*. I expect that's you, Luella, is it?'

Giggles, shrieks and whistles filled the hall as a totally astonished Niffy went forward to collect her basket.

'Happy Valentine's,' Gina called after her friend.

'Good grief,' Niffy muttered under her breath.

When she returned with the basket, she warned her friends: 'If you've all clubbed together to humiliate me, I'm going to kill you!'

'No!' Min insisted. 'This is for real.'

Gina peered over Niffy's shoulder as she tore open the little envelope and looked at the note written inside.

'*Hello, gorgeous. I'm back. See you tonight? A x*'

'A? A!! That's Angus! It can't be anyone else can it? He's back from France and he wants to see you *tonight*!'

Gina exclaimed. 'This is amazing news: he's missed you, he wants to pick up just where you left off.'

'Or ... he's no longer able to hang out with glamorous French girls so he's decided to give boring old me another whirl,' Niffy said with a face which was an odd mixture of shy, excited, anxious and amused. She obviously had no idea what to think.

'Stop it,' Min said. 'It's very exciting. I wonder where he wants to meet you?'

'Oh God, my hair,' Niffy groaned, putting her hands up to her mop, which was still dotted with weird orange patches.

'Don't worry, we'll help,' Gina said kindly.

'Here's the postman!' Mrs Knebworth called from the hallway. 'I bet he's laden down today.'

Girls now all flocked into the hallway. Sure enough the postman handed over two huge bundles of mail. Much of it was in pink and red envelopes.

'Calm!' Mrs Knebworth insisted as she took the bundles and stood over the mail table to sort them out.

She read out the names on the envelopes and anyone who happened to be in the hallway when a card was passed to them was treated to whistles and applause.

Niffy, holding her flowers, whistled the loudest when

first Gina and then Min were each handed a card, Gina's in a bright pink envelope.

Then it was the turn of all the girls to whistle and laugh when Mrs Knebworth said of one pale pink envelope, 'Oh! This one seems to be for me.'

Min had to ask Niffy sharply: 'Did you send that?'

'No. Our surprise is on its way,' she replied, shooting Gina a wink.

'Open yours, Min,' Gina instructed as she tore at her own envelope.

Min opened hers more carefully and brought out a folded sheet of graph paper. On the front of it there was a heart which had been made completely out of scribbled numbers and formulae.

'No guessing who that's from then?' Niffy said as Min blushed and giggled.

'So what has Dermot sent you?' Min asked, wanting the attention away from the card in her hands as quickly as possible.

Gina had a shop-bought card in her hand. Pink and white with gold bits. Not really Dermot's taste, she couldn't help thinking – a little too gaudy.

Had his mum bought it for him? The thought crossed her mind. Maybe he'd been too busy studying to get to the shops.

She opened the card and read out the words that had been printed with a red felt-tip pen:

'*Roses are red, roses are pink, a surprise date would be fun . . . what do you think? Sunday Feb 15. Scott Monument, Princes Street, 12 noon. Shhhhhh. Could a lad like u more? Xx*'

'Wow!' Min said. 'That sounds so romantic.'

'About time,' Gina said. 'He's been so boring about his studying. And he's spending Saturday night working in the café.'

The mobile in her pocket began to buzz.

She pulled it out, looked at the screen and said: 'Amy says Happy Valentine's, and did we all get something.'

Gina texted an update.

Back came the message: UR ALL SO LUCKY! NOTHING 4 ME?'

NO, Gina had to text back.

NEVER MIND, Amy replied.

But Gina and her friends had a feeling that she probably did mind very much. Last year four cards had arrived for Amy. She'd been the most popular girl in the year.

How could she not mind that things were so different this year?

HOW GOING IN G'GOW? Gina texted next.

BIT GLOOMY, came the reply.

'Poor old Amy,' Gina told her friends.

'Look, same card as me,' Milly from Daffodil dorm said, pointing to Gina's card and holding up her own as she walked past. 'Did you enjoy your wine?' she added in a whisper.

'Just about to,' Niffy replied.

Just then two sixth formers came in through the front door and one called out: 'Hey, Mrs K, there's something for you out on the stone steps.'

Niffy shot Min a wink.

'This is your surprise, is it?' Min asked.

'We wanted her to know how much Jaguar man could care . . . with a little encouragement,' Niffy whispered.

'Jaguar man?' Min wrinkled up her forehead. 'But didn't I tell you? He's not a date of any kind. He's her late husband's cousin.'

'Oh no!' Gina exclaimed.

Chapter Twenty-five

Amy held up a skinny gold belt. She had no idea when she'd last worn it, so she tossed it into the eBay box. This was her new policy: if she couldn't even remember wearing something, then – unless it was absolutely gorgeous and she was sure she would wear it again – into the box it had to go.

Two hours had passed and the eBay boxes were filling up. Amy wasn't just getting a sense of how much money she might make with her wardrobe sale, she was also getting an idea of just how much money she'd spent over the past few years.

Her dad had always given her a very generous amount of pocket money every month – and she'd always spent it all. Overspent, even. She actually had her own credit card, backed up by Dad's funds.

It had always made her feel good, knowing that her dad was loaded. Knowing that she could just about have everything she'd ever wanted. When snobby witches like Penny Boswell-Hackett tried to tease her about being a trashy Glaswegian whose dad ran 'sleazy' nightclubs, being able to flaunt her wealth had made Amy feel better. She'd worn real diamonds to school, designer clothes at the weekends and show-stopping dresses to the dances.

Expensive clothes, expensive jewels and envy-inducing labels had been her thing. Her armour. Her defence against any kind of hint that she wasn't good enough to be at St Jude's; that she wasn't posh enough or snobby enough.

Girls like Penny, and even Niffy, were the kind of girls whose mothers had gone to St Jude's. They felt as if they belonged.

Amy had always known that she *didn't* belong. Min and Gina, who were both foreign, never seemed to mind too much that they too didn't belong. But for Amy, it bothered her. She wanted to fit in, be a part of the school and belong.

Now that there wasn't going to be the armour of being rich, she wondered how she would manage.

She would all of a sudden be much more ordinary. She wouldn't be able to boast about her dad and his fabulous career any more, would she?

The violet silk blouse in her hands was carefully considered. She wouldn't give this away. She needed to hang on to some really good things. To be honest, she wanted to keep up the pretence of being rich for as long as possible.

As soon as she was wearing chain-store clothes and high-street shoes . . . everyone would know. Everyone would know her dad's business had failed, that she was staying on at school by a thread and she wasn't able to splash her cash about like she had done in the good old days.

She folded the blouse carefully into a box going to her gran's.

Mrs Knebworth, clutching the bottle of wine, began to walk towards Niffy and her friends.

'Uh oh,' Gina hissed.

'Told you!' Min warned.

'Stay calm,' Niffy instructed.

'Girls? Luella?' Mrs Knebworth began. 'Is this anything to do with you?'

Niffy shook her head and gave a shrug.

Min's 'no!' was of course totally innocent.

Gina's 'no way,' sounded completely convincing.

'Luella?' Mrs Knebworth asked once again, her eyebrows raised, her look very stern.

'Mrs K . . . I have washed windows, I have hoovered the tops of all the wardrobes, I have waxed the dining-room floor, I have unblocked the laundry room drains . . . do you honestly think I would play another single trick on you ever again?'

Mrs Knebworth continued to look at Niffy long and hard.

Then a smile broke out across her face. 'No,' she said finally, 'I didn't think so.'

Then, waggling the wine bottle in front of her, she said, 'Well then . . . I'll have to accept that this is possibly the sign of a whole new development.'

Min gave Niffy a horrified look. She hoped it told Niffy that now was the time to confess, right now, before things went even more haywire. But Niffy stayed silent.

A glance at her watch told Amy it was nearly two o'clock. She'd been working on her cupboard clearout for hours. And on Valentine's Day! It wasn't as if she'd forgotten that it was Valentine's Day . . . although everyone seemed to have forgotten her.

Four cards! She'd had four Valentine's cards last year.

She'd suspected at least one had been sent by her dad, but even so . . . to go from four to zero was upsetting.

There still hadn't been a word from Finn either. Niffy had said it was OK for them to go out again. Amy had emailed him twice to ask when they could see each other, but she'd heard nothing.

Every time Niffy asked about it, they both felt embarrassed. 'I can't understand it,' Niffy had mumbled the last time. 'He really liked you.'

Another tear dripped from the edge of Amy's nose. She wiped it away angrily. She didn't want to feel so sorry for herself. She really didn't. What would her dad think of her? He'd think she was being a feeble loser.

She threw the last things from the wardrobe into the boxes going to her gran's house, then bundled her duvet, pillows and sheets into big plastic bags and that was it. The room was packed up. She went and stood by the large glass window and looked out over the river. She wondered when she would next be able to look at this big, sweeping view again.

Then, making sure that all trace of her tears was gone from her face, she stepped out of her bedroom, determined to help her dad with the rest of the packing.

The airy, open living space with its huge windows,

was in chaos. Boxes, piles of books and papers and half-wrapped pictures were all over the place. Amy went over to the nearest pile of paperwork and began packing it into the nearest box.

'I don't think we'll be too much longer,' her dad called from the kitchen, where he was wrapping up glasses and brewing a fresh pot of coffee.

This was a bit optimistic, Amy couldn't help thinking. By the look of this room and the kitchen, there were still hours and hours of packing ahead.

She picked up another handful of books and papers and dumped them into the box. 'Let's just keep going,' she said and a busy forty minutes or so passed before Amy was startled out of her sad thoughts by a loud brrrrrrring on the flat's buzzer.

'The door,' her dad called out. 'That'll be the huge Valentine's delivery for you, will it? Does boy of the moment know your home address, and should I be worried?'

Amy looked up in surprise. 'There is no boy of the moment . . . I'm not expecting anything.'

'Well, let's see who it is.'

He pressed the intercom button. 'Hello?'

'Special delivery,' the voice replied.

'Come on up.'

Amy's dad grinned at her. 'Sounds very exciting.'

Amy couldn't help it, she began to grin too. She felt her heartbeat skip about a little.

It was probably nothing. It was probably just another delivery of boxes that her dad had forgotten about, or something ultra boring.

But then, maybe . . . just maybe . . . could it possibly be Finn? Was he finally going to surprise her?

They could hear the lift whirring up the ten floors towards them.

'I'm sure it's not for me,' Amy told her dad.

But he just waggled his eyebrows.

Maybe he'd done this? Maybe he'd ordered something just to cheer her up? That was the only possible explanation, wasn't it?

The doorbell ping-ed.

Her dad went to the door and opened it wide: wide enough for Amy to see an enormous bunch of bright yellow sunflowers.

Then three faces appeared from behind the flowers.

'*Surprise*!' Gina called out.

'Happy Valentine's!' Min announced.

'Your packing crew has arrived,' Niffy added.

'You shouldn't have come!' Amy kept telling her friends

as they helped her and her dad to blitz through the rest of the packing. Practised trans-Atlantic flier Gina turned out to be genius at making entire piles of stuff just disappear.

Throughout the packathon, Amy was brought up to speed with all the Valentine's news: Niffy's flowers from Angus (no!), Gina and Min's cards, Mrs Knebworth and the wine bottle.

'Unfortunately Jaguar man turns out to be her cousin,' Niffy said, pulling a face.

'No!' Amy said, looking horrified at the mistake they'd made. 'So there's no way there's anything romantic going on?'

'He's not her cousin – he's her dead husband's cousin,' Min corrected.

'Still . . . please tell me that you managed to stop her getting the bottle?' Amy asked.

'Er . . . no. Min only told us very last minute,' Niffy explained.

'Don't blame me. I keep telling you to leave her alone,' Min huffed.

'Well, anyway, she came and asked us if we had anything to do with it,' Niffy went on. 'We said that we didn't and then she looked a bit odd and said something about interesting new developments. That's when we decided we'd better get right out of her way and Gina had the brilliant idea of saying you'd phoned up in tears, and could we all go over to Glasgow to see you?'

'Oh. I see! So you're not really being nice, you just needed an escape!' Amy said, but with a smile.

'Aim,' Niffy said, smiling back, 'you know we are only here for you. It's Valentine's, we couldn't leave you here all day like a great big green gooseberry.'

Amy's dad snorted with laughter at this, and Amy's smile broke into a grin. No matter why they'd come, it was very, very comforting to have them here.

'So what time are you meeting Greg?' Amy asked Min.

Min coloured up. 'Seven o'clock, Dermot's café.'

Gina took out her phone and texted Dermot: WE ARE COMING TO YOUR CAFÉ ABOUT 7, VALENTINE, WATCH OUT!

LOOK 4WARD, VALENTINE, Dermot replied.

'And Angus?' Gina looked up at Niffy. 'Have you phoned him?'

'I don't know ...' Niffy began. 'I don't know if I really want ... What about my hair?'

'Oh, please!' Amy interrupted. 'Ever since Angus left for France, you've been mooching about like a kicked puppy. Now take my phone and ring him or else I will blooming well do it for you!'

Niffy took the mobile but just held it in her hand, as if she expected it to blow up or something.

'You have brought his number, haven't you?' Amy asked. 'Please tell me that you've done that.'

'Yeah!' Niffy huffed and then went in search of the tatty canvas shoulder bag which she carried about. 'Just don't all listen, OK? In fact, don't listen at all.'

'Fine. Go lock yourself in the bathroom,' Amy instructed. 'Phone Angus from the jacuzzi if you want to.'

'Hey, no messing with my jacuzzi,' Amy's dad teased. 'The luxury bathroom's the reason I've got someone paying me a lot of rent for this place.'

'Dad, would you mind if I went back to Edinburgh tonight?' Amy asked. 'We'll help you get everything into the van and over to Gran's, but then . . . if you could just make a little call to Mrs K and tell her we're having dinner with you and that we'll be back at the boarding house by eleven, we can then treat ourselves to a nice little evening—'

'On the tiles?' Amy's dad interrupted.

'No! There's this café and there are a few friends . . .' Amy began.

'You mean, there's this wine bar and there are these boys,' her dad translated.

'Maybe, but we are very, very good, very well-behaved St Jude's girls,' Amy wheedled, 'and haven't we been so nice to pack for you all day?'

'Get away!' Amy's dad said with a smile.

'Go on,' Amy pleaded.

'A nice, quiet wine bar? With some nice, quiet boys?' he asked.

'I'm not going to the wine bar, I'm staying in the café,' Min pointed out.

'We'll all be in the café till it shuts at nine . . .' Amy said.

Her dad took his mobile out of his pocket. 'You better be very, very good. If anything goes wrong, I will be in deep trouble with Mrs K and no man anywhere on the face of the earth wants to be in trouble with Mrs K. She is one scary lady.'

This made everyone giggle. Amy's dad turned away and went to the kitchen to call, just as Niffy came out of the bathroom.

She was blushing and smiling.

'Are you going to see him?' Amy asked.

Niffy nodded.

'Was he pleased to hear from you?'

Niffy nodded.

'Are you going to tell us anything else?' Gina asked.

Niffy shook her head and blushed some more.

Amy's dad came back into the room. 'OK, you can have your night out in Edinburgh. But you will be back at the boarding house by eleven o'clock sharp!'

Before anyone could cheer, he added: 'I didn't speak to Mrs Knebs, by the way, apparently she's not in tonight. I spoke to Miss McKinnon.'

'The Neb has gone out? On Valentine's? On a date?!' Amy wondered out loud.

It was a thrilling, horrifying prospect.

'Brave, brave man,' Amy's dad said. 'Look, forget about helping me to pack the van. I'll take you all out for a quick pizza, then drive you to the station. You'll need something filling before you go off and drink all those . . . coffees.' He raised his eyebrows.

'But, Dad,' Amy protested, 'we can't go out and get a pizza now. First of all, we have to get ready!'

'Oh – how could I be so daft?!'

Gina, Min and Niffy all looked at each other and shrugged.

'We've not brought anything to change into,' Gina pointed out.

'Better come to my room then,' Amy said with a

smile. 'I have boxes and boxes of stuff that is desperate for one last outing before it disappears.'

The four girls rushed in the direction of Amy's room with something which, to Amy's bemused dad, sounded almost like a battle-cry.

Chapter Twenty-six

Four very pretty, very dressed-up girls marching through Glasgow's Queen Street station carrying sunflowers caused a little bit of a stir at 6 p.m. on Valentine's night.

'Are you looking for a date?'

'Will I do?'

'How's about coming out with me?'

. . . were amongst the questions the girls were asked by brave passers-by.

'Are you jokin' us?' was Amy's standard, pithy response. Sometimes she even risked: 'Yeah, if Frankenstein's not available, I'll let you know.'

Everyone was dressed head to toe from Amy's beautiful wardrobe. Min was in a floaty fuchsia pink dress and black pointy boots, Gina wore skin-tight jeans with a blue satin top and lots of fake gold. Amy had been almost tempted to take the feathers out for a crazy whirl around the town, but instead she'd plumped for a sparkly red tunic over lace leggings and shiny black shoe-boots.

The most unbelievable change was in Niffy.

Amy had gelled and styled the poor blobby orange hair, Amy had clipped on earrings, applied lip-gloss, eyeliner . . . Amy had somehow coaxed Niffy into tight purple boots and a silvery grey sweater dress with a low V-back.

Niffy now looked amazing. Unbelievably different and weirdly grown up. Because she was tall, in make-up and a dress, she suddenly looked in her late teens.

She wasn't entirely happy about the purple boots though. Although they were low, they had a narrow pointy heel and she kept tripping, slipping and generally cursing Amy.

'How do you walk in these things?' she complained. 'You must be an acrobat. You're going to have bunions when you're an old lady.'

'Shut up!' Amy commanded. 'At least I'm not already an old lady . . . like certain people.'

On the train, they grabbed a table seat so they could all sit together. As the train pulled out of the station, Amy put her little patent handbag up on the table, opened the zip and brought out a small bottle of deep-pink nail varnish.

'Valentine Pink,' she announced, unscrewing the top from the bottle. 'OK, who wants to be first?'

After the forty-minute journey and a chilly fifteen-minute walk, the four dressed-up, made-up and carefully nail-varnished friends walked in through the doors of the Arts Café . . . just as soon as Amy had made last-minute hair arrangements to the nervous Min and Niffy.

'You look lovely,' she'd assured them. 'Smile, walk tall and be gorgeous.'

Gina was in front. She scanned the café and was amazed at how busy it was tonight. Just about every single table was taken and there was a queue of people at the counter.

Tea lights in red glass holders and single pink roses in tiny vases had been set out on all the tables. There were heart-shaped decorations hanging up in all the windows, and the blackboard behind the counter promised: '*Pink cupcakes, passion fruit slices and coffees made with love.*'

Gina looked around carefully. She could see Dermot – busy, busy at the coffee machine – but she couldn't see anyone else she recognized. There was a knot of boys sitting at one of the tables, but not one of them was Angus. Then someone waved from a small table in the corner.

'It's Greg!' Min said, her voice all high-pitched with nerves.

'We'll all go over and say hello,' Gina said, understanding that Min might like them all to help her break the ice.

'No sign of Angus then,' Niffy said. Her voice sounded gloomy.

'We're totally on time for Min to meet Greg,' Amy pointed out. 'You told us that Angus said seven thirty so he's still got half an hour to get here. And if he's anything up to twenty minutes late, that's acceptable.'

Once Min had been dropped off at her cosy table for two with Greg, Gina, Amy and Niffy joined the queue at the counter.

'Hi! We are totally rushed off our feet,' were Dermot's opening words as he spotted the girls. 'Must be the heart-shaped chocolate sprinkles on the top of the coffees. People can't get enough of them.'

'Hello . . . Happy Valentine's Day,' Gina began. 'Did you get my card?'

'Yeah, it was very nice. Thank you,' Dermot said, but

he was distracted, busy taking money from another customer, then sticking an order note to a mug.

'I got yours, thanks,' Gina said, but she wasn't sure if he had heard her or not. Never mind. She would get the chance to talk to him later when the rush had died down a bit.

'Isn't your dad here?' she asked.

'In the kitchen, knocking out more cupcakes,' Dermot said. 'He never, ever leaves me and Rachel here in charge on a Saturday night, but we're so busy, about to run out of food . . . and my baking's terrible, he has no choice. Big responsibility moment for me. What can I get you? Look, over there, table eleven's coming free, run over and get it and I'll bring your drinks over when I get a second.'

Once Gina, Amy and Niffy were seated, Niffy couldn't help taking another careful look around the café to see if there was any sign of Angus.

'He said seven thirty!' she reminded them.

'Don't fret,' Amy instructed.

Dermot came over with a tray. He was just about jogging, he was in such a hurry to drop off their drinks and get back to the counter.

He plonked mugs down in front of them with a pink heart-shaped marshmallow in each, picked the rose out of the vase and handed it to Gina.

'Happy Valentine's,' he said.

'Ah, the romance,' Gina teased, accepting the rose but putting it back into the vase.

'Did you all get lots of cards?' he asked Niffy and Amy.

'Niffy got flowers,' Gina pointed out.

'Yeah, from some guy who hasn't turned up yet,' Niffy grumbled. 'What is going on? What's happened to him?'

'Do you want to phone him?' Amy offered her mobile.

'No . . . not yet. Maybe in a bit.'

'Gina, I've got something for you . . .' Dermot added, turning to go back to the counter again. 'Just give me a chance. Stay put. Don't go anywhere.'

This made Gina feel a little better. He had something for her. He had actually thought about her for one second, in between maths, history, English essays and coffee orders.

'Look at Min and Greg,' Amy pointed out. 'They are so into each other. They're leaning over the table, can't take their eyes off each other, chatting away . . .'

'About quantum relativity,' Niffy added.

'Whatever rings their bell,' Amy said.

When Dermot returned to their table, he was holding a large tray and as he set it down on the table in front of them, he gave a proud: 'Da-dah.'

On the tray was a heart-shaped cake covered in pink blotchy icing which looked touchingly home-made.

'Oh, WOW!' was the group response.

'Amazing!'

'Fantastic!'

'That looks delicious,' Gina told Dermot. 'Please tell me you're going to let us eat some right now.'

'Yeah, you will share, won't you, Gina?' Niffy asked.

'Sure! Of course.'

As Dermot began to cut the cake and serve it out onto the little plates he'd brought, an extremely posh male voice boomed out from some distance away:

'There's the Nifster, her friends and even the Yank!'

With a sinking heart, Gina realized that the awful Charlie Fotheringham-whatsit and two of his friends were heading in their direction.

Chapter Twenty-seven

'Dermot, I think you'd better go back to the serving counter,' Gina hissed.

The last time Dermot and Charlie had run into each other, there had been a fight. A real fist-fight! Friends had rushed in to pull them apart, but both boys had nursed sore jaws and swollen cheeks for days afterwards.

But it was too late. Charlie and his two friends were already at the table.

'What are *you* doing here?' Dermot asked, looking up with an angry face. 'Looking for Round Two, are you?'

'You can't keep the girls all to yourself, you know, we're here to take them somewhere a bit more exciting,' Charlie said smoothly.

'We don't want to go anywhere with you!' Gina said, outraged at Charlie's suggestion. He hadn't even said hello but he was trying to get them to go with him.

Charlie just ignored this; he looked over at Niffy and said, 'Hello, Lou, I didn't recognize you. Where's your hair?'

'And your trousers?' one of his friends added.

'Don't be so rude!' Amy put in.

'We're here with a message from Angus. He's got held up having dinner with the oldsters at some friend's house . . . but we're to take you to the Victoria Street wine bar and he'll meet you there.'

'Suit yourself,' Dermot said, and with a shrug he began to walk away from the table.

Charlie leaned over, snatched up a teaspoon, filled it with a scoop of pink icing and flicked it at Dermot.

The blob of icing arced through the air and hit Dermot on the shoulder with a small splat. Gina gasped, sure that Dermot was going to swivel round, bellow at Charlie and another ugly fight would kick off – this time in the café.

Dermot paused.

He must have known something had hit him, but to Gina's relief he carried on walking. He clearly didn't want trouble, so he was being big and walking away from it.

Gina turned back to the table just in time to see the

spoonfuls of icing Niffy and Amy had launched, hit Charlie squarely in the face.

'Take that!' Niffy said.

'Yeah, you big idiot,' Amy added.

Charlie now had icing on his forehead and in his left eye.

'WHAT?!' he exclaimed.

Launching at the cake, he picked up a knife now, cut off a slice and catapulted it in Amy and Niffy's direction.

It landed right in Niffy's lap.

Furious, she stood up, scooped up two handfuls of the pink sponge cake and threw them at Charlie.

Niffy was a champion sportswoman, so one of her shots landed bang on his nose, the other smacked him in the chest. Meanwhile, the cake slice Amy had launched veered off course and hit Charlie's friend on the shoulder of the smart jacket he was wearing.

'Stop! Stop it!' Gina protested, but now a full-scale food fight was erupting.

Hands were tearing at the cake, sponge and icing was flying. There was a scream as a girl on the next-door table was hit by a stray sticky pink bullet.

The guy sitting with her stood up and demanded loudly: 'Hey! Look what you've done.'

Blobs of cake continued to fly around table eleven. A couple who'd brought their baby to sleep through their romantic coffee and cake moment were horrified when a glob of icing hit his car seat just centimetres from his tiny face.

Gina was screaming at the four to stop. Everyone close to the table was calling for a halt. The whole café was aware of the chaos going on. Even Greg and Min were interrupted and looked over in concern. But the fight didn't stop until Dermot, closely followed by his beetroot-faced dad, marched over.

'Get out!' Dermot yelled, taking a hold of the back of Charlie's jacket. 'Get out and don't ever come back!'

He pushed Charlie in the direction of the door and glared at the other boys with him.

Charlie glared back, his lips pulled into a tight line.

He scooped off the cake plastered to his face and flicked it disdainfully onto the floor.

'OUT!' Dermot's dad repeated furiously. The entire café had come to a standstill. Everyone was staring at the cake criminals in silence. The cosy Valentine's atmosphere was well and truly shattered.

The three boys began to head for the door as the girls sat meekly back down in their seats.

'Sorry . . .' Gina began. 'We'll help you clean up. I'm so sorry,' she repeated.

'Did you not hear what I said?' Dermot's livid, red-faced dad asked. 'GET OUT!'

For a moment the girls just stared in horror. But Dermot's dad did not exactly look like he was in the mood for a debate.

Quickly Amy, Niffy and Gina snatched up their bags and began to follow Charlie and his friends out.

Gina looked beseechingly at Dermot. Couldn't he step in? Couldn't he save them from this humiliation?

Dermot just glared furiously back.

'*Guys?!*'

As Gina, Niffy and Amy began to walk away from the café, following Charlie and co down the street, they heard Min's voice calling after them.

'Guys? Where are you going?' Min asked as her friends turned to her.

'Oh, Min, sorry!' Amy apologized. 'With all that drama up there, we forgot about you.'

'You got kicked out of Dermot's café!' Min stated the obvious, but it was just so shocking that she had to say it out loud.

'Yeah,' Gina said sadly.

'Bit tricky . . . with you on your date,' Niffy pointed out.

'Where are you going?' Min asked.

Charlie heard this and told her: 'Victoria Street wine bar, it's just round the corner. Are you going to come too?'

'No,' Min replied. She didn't like Charlie. He'd once tried to snog her when she hadn't wanted him to at all.

'We'll meet you outside the café in an hour,' Amy suggested.

The girls all had to travel back to the boarding house together that night or else the cover story that they'd all been having dinner with Amy's dad would not sound at all convincing.

'OK. But don't drink much. I'm not going back to the boarding house with you if you're all drunk,' Min warned.

'As if,' Gina replied.

'C'mon,' Charlie urged, 'or else the fun is never going to start.'

Min headed back into the café as her three friends joined the boys on the short walk to the wine bar.

'So who are your pals? You might as well introduce us.' Niffy tapped Charlie on the shoulder.

'Oh . . . I see! You want to be friends now, after you've covered us all in gloop,' Charlie complained, but he stopped and turned to face the three girls.

'This is Freddy' – he introduced the blond-haired guy on his left – 'and this is Phil. Meet Lou, Finn's sister, Amy and . . .' He paused; maybe for once he wasn't going to call Gina by the hated 'Yank' nickname.

'Gina,' Charlie said with effort. 'She's from California and she has shockingly bad taste in boyfriends.

OK now, huddle round, relax, try and look old enough to be here,' he instructed in his bossy way as they walked into the wine bar. 'What's everyone drinking? I have a wallet full of pocket money and a fake ID, so enjoy.'

Niffy took off her jacket and revealed the full extent of her cake damage.

Her neck was decorated with a streak of pink icing. Blobs of icing and sponge were stuck to her shoulders and the front of the fluffy grey dress.

'Oh, mince!' Amy exclaimed. 'Come to the bathroom with me, we have to get you sorted.'

'And you.' Niffy pointed to the large patch of pink right in the middle of Amy's chest.

But before they could leave Charlie's huddle, a broad-shouldered figure bounded up to the group.

It took Niffy a moment to realize who she was looking at. No! Despite the overgrown hair, the different clothes and the outdoorsy suntan . . . it really was Angus. The boy she'd been so mad about last year. She hadn't seen him for months, but now he was right here looking at her with something close to astonishment on his face.

'Nif!' he exclaimed, his arms held wide. 'Nif? Is that really you?'

Niffy stroked the back of her neck and turned her gaze to the floor, because all at once she felt strange and shy.

'You've cut off all your hair!'

'Yeah,' she said.

'You're wearing a dress!'

Niffy just gave a little snorty laugh.

'What do you think?' she asked, looking into his friendly face.

'I think you look good enough to eat,' Angus declared.

He threw his arms round her and to the shock of not just Niffy, but also Amy and Gina who were riveted on this little reunion scene, he gave her neck a lick.

He must have struck icing because he declared: 'You taste delicious too.'

Chapter Twenty-eight

Niffy knew she was awake, because she was sitting in the back of a taxi speeding towards the boarding house, but she felt as if she was in a blurry dream.

Her lips felt numb and tingly from all the kissing she and Angus had done in a dark corner of the wine bar. She felt as if her face, neck and shoulders were all covered with him . . . probably even smelled of him.

Seeing him again had been much more fantastic than she'd even imagined.

Min was sitting quietly in the taxi beside her with an equally dreamy look on her face. Obviously the Valentine's date with Greg had gone very well. In her hand, Min was holding the pink rose from the vase on their table.

Only Gina and Amy were talking. Amy was busy getting mints out of her handbag and giving one to everyone. Then she brought out a little bottle of perfume and told everyone to spray themselves, so that any stray wine bar fumes would be well and truly zapped.

'My dad drove us over here tonight and took us to the Taj Mahal restaurant. Then he put us in this taxi because he had to head back to Glasgow. OK? Are we all clear? That's the script and we're all sticking to it,' she explained.

'The Neb isn't in though, remember?' Gina said. 'We'll be fine.'

'The Neb wasn't in at five when my dad called,' Amy reminded her. 'Things change. We need to be prepared.' She held up her perfume bottle and gave one last squirt.

'Eeek,' Min said as Amy hit her right in the eye.

'Sorry!' Amy quickly passed her a tissue.

In the boarding-house sitting room, Miss McKinnon was on the sofa watching TV with some of the younger girls.

'Hi, did you have a nice time?' she asked as the four came into the room to sign in.

'We had a great meal, thanks, and it was so nice of everyone to come over to Glasgow today and help me . . .' Amy began. 'But it was hard to pack up the flat.'

'Poor old you,' Miss McKinnon sympathized.

Amy didn't want to say any more; there were other people in the room. This was still a situation she was working out how to talk about. She didn't know yet how open she wanted to be.

'Where's Mrs Knebworth?' Niffy couldn't resist asking.

'Oh . . .' Miss McKinnon glanced at her watch and looked almost surprised. 'She went out for dinner, but I'm expecting her back any moment now.'

'A friend or a date?' Niffy risked.

'Girls, I couldn't possibly comment!' came Miss McKinnon's reply.

Niffy had taken off her borrowed Amy clothes, she'd been to the bathroom and washed off the Amy make-up and probably all the particles of Angus that had been clinging to her. She'd considered not washing her face. She had actually considered not washing her face or her neck where he'd kissed her, just to keep some part of him still with her. But then she'd told herself off for being such a lovesick puppy.

Now, in her white-and-blue checked pyjamas (old ones of Finn's), she glanced at herself in the mirror and thought she looked just like herself again, rather than the older, sophisticated girl she'd been for a few hours tonight.

It was kind of OK, being herself again.

Even her short-haired self.

Hadn't Angus told her he liked the dress and make-up but he liked her in 'jodhpurs and horse dung' just as much?

Niffy lifted the corner of her duvet and eased her long legs into bed. As her feet travelled down the cool sheets towards the very end of the mattress, she felt . . . something.

She put her toe slowly down again. Yikes! There was definitely something down there. It was hard, but slightly furry. She touched it with her toe again and thought that it might actually have moved.

Niffy whipped back the duvet and gave a horrified screech. A huge, furry spider, black with terrifying looking yellow and orange circles on its back was nestled at the bottom of her bed.

'AAAAAAAAAAAAAAAH!' she screamed again, expecting the spider to scurry off and hide itself.

'EVACUATE!!!!' she yelled, wanting everyone out of the dorm and the door shut against this hideous beast.

The spider looked deadly. It looked totally venomous.

'Min!' Niffy shrieked, sure that Min somehow had something to do with this. Min travelled from South Africa every term. Wasn't that where all the worst spiders lived?

'OUT! OUT!' Niffy shouted. 'Huge spider! Mega spider! Got to get OUT!'

'Where?' Amy wanted to know.

'Just get out, all of you!' Niffy ordered. She was already at the door.

She pulled it open, ran out and slapped straight into Mrs Knebworth.

'Sorry,' Niffy said automatically, but immediately followed this with, 'HELP! We have a great big, massive hairy spider problem in there.'

'Really?' Mrs Knebworth's eyebrows shot up. 'This isn't another of your little jokes, Luella Nairn-Bassett?'

'NO!' Niffy said, feeling panicked.

'I'm not going to go in there and get hit in the face with exploding ink or itching powder or something equally childish?'

'No, no,' Niffy said, sounding genuinely scared. 'Will you get out of there?' she urged her friends, who still didn't seem to be taking this very seriously.

'Where is this monster?' Mrs Knebworth asked.

'In my bed, at the foot of it.'

'Well, I'll have to go and take a look,' Mrs Knebworth said.

'No, I don't think so. I think we should call the police or the RSPCA or the zoo or . . . who are you supposed to call in a deadly animal emergency?'

'Calm down, Luella,' Mrs Knebworth insisted. 'I'm just going to go and take a look.'

Gina, Amy and Min, now a little more infected by Niffy's panic, were standing in the doorway too. Min was standing on tiptoes.

'What colour was it?' she asked. Living in South Africa, she had been taught how to recognize dangerous spiders in kindergarten.

'Black with orange and yellow circles . . .' Niffy replied.

'Orange and yellow?' Min repeated with concern.

'And it was huge!' Niffy widened her hands to demonstrate.

Mrs Knebworth was right up at the bed now.

'Careful,' Niffy warned.

'That sounds like a tarantula . . . but over here?' Min said with astonishment.

'Oh!' Mrs Knebworth gasped.

Everyone else gasped too and shrank back from the doorway.

'Like this?' Mrs Knebworth asked, and for a split second the huge black spider dangled from her hand before she launched it into the air at the girls.

All four screamed with fright.

The spider hit Niffy right in the chest. But it wasn't until it fell onto her foot, was kicked off and landed several metres away in the hall that she realized it was dead. As she inched forward to take a closer look, she realized something else . . . it was made of rubber!

Now turning in a fury to her dorm-mates, she was about to storm questions at them when something else occurred to her: Mrs Knebworth was sitting at the foot of her bed, laughing fit to burst.

As Niffy walked slowly and furiously into the room, her hands balled into fists, her Angus daydreams well and truly forgotten, Mrs Knebworth looked up at her.

She lifted off her glasses and wiped at the tears of laughter which were forming there.

'Got you!' she said.

All the way down the hall, Mrs Knebworth was still laughing.

Chapter Twenty-nine

On Sunday morning, Gina tapped lightly at the door of Mrs Knebworth's sitting room.

'Come in,' boomed the familiar voice.

'Er . . . Mrs Knebworth,' Gina began. She looked at the housemistress carefully. After last night's spider incident, Mrs Knebworth didn't seem quite as knowable as she had before.

'Do you remember we spoke about me going off to meet Dermot for lunch today?'

'Oh yes!' Mrs Knebworth looked up. 'Yes, of course. Have a nice lunch and . . . you can stay out till five if you want to. The exams are over, so there's nothing to worry about for a while. Have fun,' she urged, 'but take your mobile and, obviously, come home in a taxi. It'll be getting dark by five.'

'OK!' Gina smiled gratefully.

As she hurried to get her coat, pull on her boots and

apply just another little layer of blush and gloss, she checked her mobile anxiously again.

She'd texted Dermot three times since last night.

She'd apologized again and told him she was still going to go along at twelve, just as the Valentine's card had suggested.

But there had been no reply. Nothing at all.

Still, Gina was going to go. This was Dermot – he couldn't possibly be angry with her for long. It just wasn't like him. She was absolutely sure that he would show up.

It was their first proper date in weeks because of all the studying. And it was Valentine's weekend. He couldn't blame her for the cake fight: she hadn't invited Charlie to the café, plus she'd tried to stop everyone who'd been involved.

Dermot wouldn't let her down. Maybe there was just some problem with his phone. He would be there. She knew it. And if he wasn't there, she told herself as she buttoned up her short coat, she would just take the bus out to his house and make up with him.

Way at the back of her mind was another thought. She kept trying to push it away, but every now and again it bubbled up again. That thought was – if it didn't work out with Dermot, maybe she would accept Callum's offer and go out on a date with him. No. She pushed the thought away again.

Dermot. This was all about making up with Dermot and getting back to where they were before the cake fight, the exams and the awkward hand-on-boob incident.

Gina took a bus into the centre of town, then walked the last short stretch towards the looming Scott monument.

The ornate, gothic building housed a huge marble statue of Sir Walter Scott underneath a giant tower which looked oddly like a church steeple without the church. She'd never been inside, but she did know that there was a long winding spiral staircase which took visitors up to the viewing platform at the top.

As she walked along the pavement towards the building, she began to look out for Dermot. It was a clear, cold day. He'd probably be bundled into his big, tweedy overcoat: the one he'd worn to meet her mom last year. Big mistake.

Her mom had wrinkled up her nose at first sight, as if she could practically smell that the coat had come from a charity shop. Her mom had not exactly 'got'

Dermot. She hadn't found his jokes funny and she had worried that he and Gina were just a little too close for comfort.

Maybe they had been very close back then. Now, Gina wasn't so sure. With all his time taken up with studying . . . with his looming exams in the summer . . . with the tingle gone right out of his kisses . . . Gina wasn't sure how close they were any more. She needed to see him today and find out. The Scott monument felt like a make-or-break date.

Even in February, there were plenty of tourists milling about Prince's Street Gardens: taking photos, consulting maps and guidebooks. She heard American accents and felt a little pin-prick of homesickness. Most of the time, thoughts of her family and home were at the back of her mind, but now they were jolted forward. It was a full eight weeks before she'd be home again. It was a long time. Her little brother Menzie would look shockingly different and she'd realize how much time had passed since she'd last seen him.

Gina walked all round the base of the monument and scanned the benches and paths nearby. Dermot wasn't here. He definitely wasn't here.

She checked her watch and then her mobile just to

make sure she had the time right. Both told her it was 12:03. So he wasn't exactly late. But still, she could feel her heart sinking.

She checked her phone to see if there was a message. Nothing . . . but it was too early to worry, she told herself. Just because he wasn't here at noon exactly, didn't mean that he wasn't going to come. Right?

He'd been a few minutes late before. In fact, he was often a few minutes late. He always had to take a bus into town from his home and the bus service was unreliable. She would wait. She would pull up her coat collar, stand right here in this very visible spot and wait. If he wasn't here by twenty past twelve, then she would call him and find out what was happening. But she didn't want to call before then . . .

Whump!!

Something smacked very hard against her back. Arms grabbed round her waist, squeezed tight and lifted her off the ground.

WHAT!!!

Gina would have yelled out if the breath hadn't been hugged right out of her.

As soon as her feet were back on the ground again, she wheeled around angrily, determined to tell him off for being such a goofball.

'Der—' she began, but the rest of his name stuck in her throat.

Because there, standing right behind her, his hands still around her waist, a wickedly mischievous grin across his face was: Callum.

Callum??

CALLUM!

Her heart began to race in her chest. What was this? What was this about? Was he here instead of Dermot? Was he bringing a message from Dermot? Why was this happening?

'Hello,' Callum said.

Gina just stared at him, too stunned to speak.

'Hello,' he repeated. 'You look a bit surprised.'

'Yeah,' Gina managed.

'Oh.' His hands dropped from her sides. 'Didn't you work out you were meeting *me* here?'

Gina shook her head.

'Did you think you were meeting . . . er . . . someone else here?'

Gina nodded.

'Oh.'

'How was I supposed to know?' Gina asked.

Callum, despite the cheeky grin and raised eyebrows, seemed to turn just slightly pink at this question.

'But . . . I gave you such an obvious clue,' he said.

'Huh?'

'In the card . . .'

'Huh?' Gina repeated. She had no idea what he was talking about.

'Could a lad . . .' Callum began, but tailed off, looking totally embarrassed.

'Like you more?' Gina finished the question for him. She was starting to enjoy just how pink the cool and collected Callum was turning.

'That spells out my name,' he said, turning his attention to a paper cup on the path and giving it a little kick.

'Oh,' Gina said. 'Oh! Could A Lad . . . I geddit.' She began to giggle.

'Bloody hell,' Callum said, sticking his hands into his jeans pockets, 'I thought you were supposed to be clever!'

This came with another cheeky grin.

Gina's eyes met his.

Now, she could feel a blush all of her own starting up.

'Well . . . here we are,' Callum began. 'Have you been up this thing before?' He poked his thumb in the direction of the monument.

For a moment Gina hesitated.

As soon as she said 'no', he was going to convince her to go up, wasn't he?

Did she want to go up the Scott monument with Callum? Did she want to hang out with Callum for a few hours today? Even though he was not her boyfriend . . . she had a perfectly nice boyfriend all of her own, who was about to get a whole load of strange text messages he wouldn't understand.

And . . . if Callum had sent the card, well then, that meant that Dermot hadn't sent her a Valentine, or made any kind of romantic date arrangement for today.

'C'mon,' Callum said, and he bumped his shoulder playfully against hers. 'I won't bite,' he added.

He flashed white teeth at her as he grinned.

No, he wouldn't bite, but he did look kind of hungry. His eyes weren't moving from her face.

'Well . . .'

'Go on,' he urged.

'Why did you want me to come here?' she risked. 'You know I'm going out with Dermot.'

'Yes . . . but Dermot's very busy. He's trying to get into Edinburgh Uni and you definitely look like the kind of girl who needs lots of attention. I'd quite like to be the person giving you some attention.'

This was very flattering.

'C'mon . . .' he wheedled again. 'We're just being tourists. I'm just being your tour guide . . . there's no harm in it.'

'OK, then,' Gina agreed.

'Great. I'll get the tickets,' he offered and they began to walk towards the booth.

Callum was really fit, Gina couldn't help thinking as she trailed several steps behind him, up and up the endless winding staircase.

While she tried not to pant with effort, he was chatting as he bounded up the steps. As she glanced up, she could see the rear view of his slim body, clad in dark, tight jeans and a black leather jacket, collar turned up against the cold.

'Do you play a lot of sport?' she asked, trying not to wheeze.

'Yeah. Football. On the school team,' came his reply. 'What about you?'

'They try to make me play hockey at St Jude's, but I suck.'

He turned to face her. 'Mmmm, short skirts, though,' he said with an eyebrow waggle.

'They're sludge-green with woollen socks,' she said with a smile. 'It's really not a good look, trust me.'

He held out his hand. 'I'll pull you up,' he offered.

She accepted gratefully, slipping her hand into his. His felt warm and took hold of hers firmly.

Now they were hurrying up the steps together, Gina feeling a fresh surge of energy at the prospect of reaching the top.

Light broke into the dark stairwell and then they were both up and out on the viewing platform.

As Gina looked around at the view, she couldn't help exclaiming: 'Wow! Awesome.'

'Awesome? That's sweet,' Callum said.

He hadn't let go of her hand. Gina was marvelling at the views right over the rooftops and buildings and out to the hills and sparkling blue sea beyond. But it wasn't the views that were making her heart thud.

Callum was still holding her hand. He was standing right beside her, almost pressed in against her side.

Gina looked at the view, then she glanced at the other people on the platform, anything to take her mind off this boy standing so close to her and making her heart jump just about into her throat.

Callum turned towards her. He was bending closer. Maybe, for a moment, she thought he was going to whisper something in her ear. But then, no, he was moving his face in towards hers.

She had a moment to decide.

If she wanted to pull back, this was it. She would have to do it now.

But her eyes were on his lips, and the very white teeth, and more than anything, Gina wanted to see what kissing him was going to be like.

Then his lips were pressed up against hers. His eyelashes were brushing against her cheeks. And she could feel a breathless, nervy excitement shoot all the way from the pit of her stomach down to the toes in her shoes.

Callum was kissing her!

She and Callum were *kissing*, right here in plain view . . . Thoughts of Dermot seemed to flash before her eyes. But the arms around her waist pulled her in tightly.

She was kissing someone different. Someone whose mouth felt strange and new, whose smell was . . . OK, a little heavy on the overpowering aftershave, but still, new. Different. Other.

Gina thought she might forget to breathe with excitement.

She let her eyes open a little; she saw Callum's

inky-black hair and pale skin. He was totally gorgeous.

This was all tingle. Totally one hundred per cent tingly.

It didn't stop.

She didn't let it stop. When there was a hint that he was pulling back, she moved towards him.

Long, thrilling moments went past. But finally they were going to have to break apart and say something. Look at each other. Acknowledge this.

She leaned back, feeling Callum's arms firmly interlocked behind her back.

She looked into his face. He was smiling with his eyebrows raised.

He looked just a little bit smug. His cheeky grin seemed to say that he'd known all along that this was how it was going to go.

'Whew!' he said.

'Yeah,' she replied.

Before Gina had even noticed, Callum had slipped his mobile from his pocket and was holding it up above them.

'Smile!' he instructed, then clicked the photo as he drew her towards him for another kiss.

Chapter Thirty

After assembly on Monday morning, as the Upper Fifth were filing out of the hall, the physics teacher, Mrs Wilson, spotted Min and pulled her to one side.

'Asimina!' she called out with a friendly smile.

'Hi, Mrs Wilson,' Min smiled back. Of all the teachers at St Jude's, Mrs Wilson was her favourite, and physics was her best subject.

'The exam results are up in the corridor outside the staff room. Have you had a chance to see them yet?'

Min looked surprised. 'Really? Already?!' she asked. 'No . . . no, I haven't.'

'Well go, Min, go and take a look. If you're quick you'll get a look before the first lesson.'

Now Min looked almost frightened.

'Don't be silly!' Mrs Wilson said. 'You've done incredibly well. I shouldn't say, you should go and look for yourself. But I will tell you that you've got one hundred per cent in your physics papers. And I made that exam tough, you know.'

'A hundred per cent?' Min repeated. 'Really? Are you sure?'

'Yes, I marked the thing myself. I am sure. Now go, go look at the board. Quick!'

Min didn't need to be told again. Turning on her heel, she began to sprint up the huge wooden staircase towards the staff-room corridor.

As soon as she reached the place, she began to scan the big white pages pinned to the cork notice board for her name.

'Sallih, Sargent . . . Singupta,' she whispered under her breath, following the names down the list.

'English A, Maths A, History A, French A?'

She had to pause and double-check that. An A in French?! She was rubbish at French compared to her friends.

Chemistry A, Biology A, Physics A with a star. Star? Was that the 100% result Mrs Wilson had been talking about. Good grief!

'So? How well have you done?'

Min felt a hand clap her on the shoulder, and she turned to see that Niffy had followed her into the corridor.

'Not bad,' she said modestly. 'I've managed to get As in everything.' She kept the precious star to herself. She didn't like to boast.

'Not bad?' Niffy teased. 'The girl gets an A in everything and says she's done not bad!' She began to scan the board for her name. More girls were coming down the corridor now. Word about the results board must have got out. The bell rang for the first class of the day, but no one paid it any attention – everyone was desperate to see how they'd done.

Min and Niffy were beginning to feel jostled by the crowd building up behind them.

'All right,' Niffy said. 'No need to get your knickers in a twist, we'll be out of your way in a second.'

'What about you? What did you get?' Min asked her friend.

'Bs . . . ooops, a C in history . . . and an A in maths. Not too bad then . . .'

'Let's take a look.' Amy and Gina were behind them now.

As Amy's eyes scanned the assortment of As, Bs and Cs she'd scored, she heard Penny B-H's plummy tones ringing out in the corridor.

She'd managed to keep out of Penny's way for some time now and really, she liked it that way. She could always come back and check the board thoroughly at break time. So she turned and tried to make her way out of the corridor in the opposite direction from Penny.

'Not so fast, Amy McCorquodale,' Penny said, her voice travelling in clear, ringing tones across the large huddle of thirty or so Upper Fifths all scrambling for a look at the results.

'I'd just like to know if your dad is Glasgow nightclub owner, Gary McCorquodale? The same Gary McCorquodale who featured in a little news story in the *Herald* on Saturday. Apparently his "empire" of clubs is finished: almost all of them are up for sale due to financial "irregularities". So is that him, then?'

Penny was standing right in front of Amy, one hand on her hip as she gazed coolly down.

All the girls in front of the boards had fallen silent. Everyone was straining to hear what was going to come next.

Amy was looking at Penny closely. Penny had a face which could have been pretty, except the features were just a little blunted, her nose was too snub, her chin was too small and her pale skin was lost in a blur of freckles. Her brown, curly hair had an unflatteringly short fringe across the forehead. Yes, Penny could have been pretty, but instead, she just looked mean. Her eyes were a cool grey-blue and they looked odd. Something was not right about the eyes . . . it was the lashes.

The brown lashes were missing. They'd been cut so short on both eyes that they were hardly there at all.

Amy glanced over at Piggy and Weasel, who were now on either side of Penny. As usual, Penny never had the guts to be rude to Amy unless she had her support team crowded around her.

'Hmmm?' Penny said, sounding impatient. 'So has your dad gone bust, Amy? Are you about to leave St Jude's? Where, let's face it, a Glaswegian like you, was never going to fit in.'

'Shut up!' Niffy piped up.

'It's OK,' Amy said. 'Let her have her little moment. Yeah, my dad's having some difficulties. His business partner wasn't all that he was supposed to be. My dad's squared up to it and is trying to put it right just as soon as he can.

'That's business, Penny, some ups, some downs. You've got to be brave and take the rough with the smooth if you want to get anywhere. My dad started with nothing. Less than nothing, but he worked all the way up to be a multi-millionaire. He's not worried about a little set-back like this; he can work his way up all over again. He's only thirty-three, for Pete's sake.'

There was an audible gasp from the crowd.

'And don't even think I'm going anywhere,' she added, sounding much more defiant and confident than she really felt. 'I'm going to be right here at St Jude's for the rest of my school life, bugging the tits off of you!'

Amy decided to leave it there and make a break for it, so she turned and began to speed walk in the direction of the English classroom.

'What's wrong with her eyes?' she hissed at Niffy as they hurried down the corridor together. 'She doesn't seem to have any eyelashes left.'

'Oh . . . well . . . I might have put a little drop of superglue in her mascara.'

'You did NOT!'

Chapter Thirty-one

'That is a gorgeous belt, Five ninety-nine? What a total bargain. You know it looks just like Gucci. Really,' Amy said, curling the red and black patent plastic into a spiral. Then she reached down underneath the counter for a bag and took the ten-pound note from the shopper.

When the till kerrrrrr-chinged open, Amy put the note into the correct slot, drew out the change and tore off the receipt.

'There you go: four pounds and a penny change to you. You've got twenty-eight days to return it, in perfect condition, but I know you won't!'

This was fun. This was much more fun than she could possibly have imagined. In fact, it was just as much fun being on this side of the till as being on the other. *And* she was getting paid ... and in a few months' time, she'd be entitled to a staff discount of her very own. At River Island!

Who'd have ever thought she'd want a staff discount at River Island? But she did. There was loads of great stuff in there. In fact, Amy was rapidly reviewing her opinion that only losers shopped in chain stores. During her first day in the job, she'd seen some very smart customers come in – ones with lovely bags and posh boots, who clearly did their top-up shopping right here on the high street.

So far, she'd made £467 with her eBay wardrobe sale. She was planning to work every Saturday during term time and then hopefully she could get longer hours at the Glasgow branch during the holidays.

Amy was now putting money *in* to her bank account. Before, she'd only ever taken money out. And putting it in felt better. It really did. Plus, she had a feeling that she was going to be much more careful with money she'd earned than with money her dad had given to her.

As she glanced up to see who her next customer was, a grin crossed her face. Niffy and Gina were walking towards her till, Gina holding a pair of earrings in her hand.

'Hi!' Gina exclaimed.

'How's it going?' Niffy asked.

'Great. But you'll have to be quick. No chit-chatting on the job!'

'Is it really OK?' Gina asked.

'I'm having a ball,' Amy assured her.

'What if Penny comes in?' Niffy wanted to know. 'Have you thought about that.'

'Yeah, I have actually. I'm going to tell her that hey, broke is the new rich, bling is dead. Get used to it. Make do and mend . . . or in my case, good-bye shopping at Harvey Nichols, hello working in River Island.'

'Nice,' Niffy exclaimed.

'So, are these for your date tonight?' Amy asked Gina as she scanned the earrings and popped them into a bag.

'Maybe . . .'

'With Dermot? Or with Callum?' Amy asked. 'We just don't know these days.'

'Don't,' said Gina. 'I'm feeling bad enough.'

'Which one is it?' Amy asked again.

'I'm going to meet Dermot at the cinema tonight . . . and Callum thinks I'm going to break up with him . . . with Dermot,' Gina explained.

'Thinks?'

'Well, he knows. That's what I've told Callum I'm going to do.'

Amy looked at Gina seriously now. 'Is that what you want to do? I mean really, *really*? This is Dermot we're talking about. The lovely, lovely Dermot. Once you let him go, there will be a crowd, a flock, no a stampede at the café door. You won't get him back, Gina. He'll be buried under an avalanche of desperate girls.'

'The lovely, lovely Dermot,' Gina said. 'That's the problem. We're like this comfortable old couple already. Everybody knows about us – everybody's watching us and talking about us and wondering when we're going to break up or have sex or get married. I feel claustrophobic. And it's not just that . . . he's had no time for me . . . '

'It was the exams.' Niffy defended him.

'No Valentine's card . . . ' Gina protested.

'You got a cake,' Amy reminded her.

'His dad baked the cake. It was probably for the café. There was no card, there was no date. There is no sparkle. He's just all about studying and revising and working in the café and saving up and it's totally boring. Callum is fun. He's exciting . . . Tomorrow, he's taking me to a funfair. I like the fact that I don't know him. It's very exciting getting to know him.'

'Poor Dermot.' Amy had to sympathize as she took Gina's money. 'He's mad about you. He's going to feel so bad. He's going to regret every second he spent with his books and not with you. And you're going to dump him for his best friend!'

'He's not his best friend. He's *one* of his friends.' Gina tried to make it sound better than she knew it was.

'Poor, poor Dermot.' Amy shook her head. 'He's forgiven you about the cake fight, you've convinced him you were texting a friend about last Sunday, and now he thinks you're going on a lovely make-up cinema trip. Poor Dermot.'

'We have to go,' Gina said, stuffing her change into her purse.

'Don't wear those boots or those leggings,' Amy called out after her.

'Why not?'

'You look too cute. Go looking plain . . . ugly, even.'

As Gina walked towards the queue of people waiting outside the Filmhouse cinema, she felt properly nervous.

Dermot was the first boy she'd really got to know well, her first real 'boyfriend'.

Dumping the guys she'd been on one or two squishy

and embarrassing dates with back home had not exactly been hard. She'd just sent them a text saying: SORRY, I'M BUSY, and they had got the message. But this . . . this was going to be different. This was going to be difficult.

There he was – she saw with a start – already in the queue, waving at her. She waved back and set a smile in place. Should she watch the film? she wondered. Should she tell him now, in the queue? Or should they watch the film together and should she tell him afterwards?

All the way here she'd been wondering which would be better and she still hadn't decided.

'Hello, Gina, how are you doing?' Dermot called over to her.

She walked towards him and accepted the hug and kiss on the lips, but she pulled back before it could get any more intimate.

'Hi,' she said, and gave him a smile which she hoped didn't look too sympathetic.

'Gina, Gina.' Dermot was smiling at her. He shook his head. 'It's been ages since we went out. I'm sorry it's been so long.'

'The cake disaster . . . I am so, so sorry about the cake disaster.'

'The Valentine's Day massacre? Yeah . . . that wasn't great. If I ever see that Charlie prat, I'll break his neck. Seriously, I'll put the prick on crutches.'

'What's going to happen when your dad sees me?' Gina wondered, forgetting for a moment that she was supposed to be breaking up with Dermot and never seeing him or his family again.

'I don't know. You, Amy and the Charlie gang are currently banned from the café. Dad is actually going to throw you out if you turn up again . . . well, so he says. But his bark has always been worse than his bite.'

'It must be kinda difficult living with someone with so many anger issues.'

'Anger issues?' Dermot began to laugh. 'That's good, I like that. Nice way of putting it.'

Gina couldn't help it, she began to laugh too.

She looked up at Dermot's friendly and familiar face. His arm was round her shoulder and suddenly she wasn't sure.

Did she really want to go out with Callum more? Did she really not want to spend any more time with Dermot? Not want to get to know him even better?

'What's the film?' she asked.

'Ah . . . an experimental Polish biopic about the head

of an asylum. Supposed to be fascinating. The *Guardian* gave it four stars.'

See, that was so Dermot. He'd asked her out to an experimental Polish biopic.

'Romantic.' Gina giggled and took his arm. 'Smoochy.'

As she caught Dermot's smile, she knew she wanted to kiss him. Very much. If she could just kiss him properly and see if the tingle was back, then she would know she should stay with him. She reached her face up towards his, but he moved back and her kiss landed on his jaw.

'Well, if you want smooch,' he said, 'you could obviously go to the rom-com showing on screen two. If you look closely, over there in the queue, you can just make out Min. But her face is hidden because she is busy licking Greg's lips off.'

'What?!'

Gina looked over in surprise. 'I didn't know they were going to the cinema tonight.'

'She's got her secrets then . . . just like you.'

As Dermot said this, he tapped Gina lightly on the nose.

Then his face turned all serious and Gina felt her heart begin to thud.

'Dermot . . . there's something we need to talk about . . .' she began, her voice sounding all choked and tense.

'I think you mean some*one*,' Dermot said.

'Someone?' Gina repeated, barely above a whisper. 'Do you know?'

'Do you want to tell me what I should know?'

Even in the dim street-lighting, Gina could see that Dermot's face looked different. There was an embarrassed flush to it and he kept looking up, avoiding her eye, and he seemed to be clenching and unclenching his jaw.

'Ummmm . . .' Gina stalled. She looked down at the ground and felt Dermot's arm drop from her shoulder. 'I got a Valentine's card and I thought it was from you, inviting me on a date. I went and it turned out to be . . . Callum.'

She looked at Dermot pleadingly. Until she'd met him here tonight, she'd been certain that she wanted this friendship to end. But now she was almost certain that she didn't. She really, really liked him.

How could she have forgotten that?

Dermot looked upwards and the muscle in his jaw flicked some more.

'He was really good fun,' Gina said in a low voice.

Dermot drew his breath in sharply at this, making Gina feel like she'd hit him.

'And well, we . . .' She was about to say 'kissed', but decided that was totally unfair. 'We thought at the time . . . that we might like to see each other again,' she said instead, feeling like a total traitor now.

'Well, that's nice. I'm very happy for you both,' Dermot said, his voice sounding strained.

'Dermot! I came here to . . . to . . .'

'Break up with me?'

'I don't know . . .' she admitted. 'I thought that's what I wanted, but now I don't think I do.'

She put her hand over his, but he moved it away.

'You've been snogging someone I consider a friend, behind my back,' he said.

'What?!' Gina gasped, astonished that she'd been found out.

'Yeah. Callum showed a picture to someone else and word got around . . .' Looking directly at her, he added in a low voice, 'There's a St Jude's boarder in the year above you who also considers herself his girlfriend. You might just like to know that.' Dermot was trying to sound angry, but he just sounded upset, which was making Gina's insides squeeze with regret.

'What?!' she repeated.

She'd made a huge mistake. A terrible mistake. She had to make up with Dermot, right now.

'I'm sorry,' she said. 'I'm sorry . . . but you've been so busy. You've not had any time for me.'

'I was studying. I don't think that makes it OK for you to go off and snog my friend.'

'Dermot, please, I'm sorry.'

They stood looking at each other in silence for several moments. The queue moved forward, but Gina knew they couldn't go and watch the film.

'I thought I was going to meet you. I didn't know it was going to be him,' she tried again.

'Well, let's see . . . did you know you were kissing Callum? Or did he blindfold you and disguise his voice?'

Gina didn't want to reply to this.

She looked around and her eye fell on Min again. She and Greg had stopped kissing and were chatting to each other. They looked so happy.

But over here in the Gina and Dermot queue, everything was totally confused, snarled up, and she had a horrible feeling they were not going to get over this.

The feeling was growing, like dread, in the pit of her stomach.

'Dermot, I'm sorry,' she said again, and began to feel a lump build in the back of her throat.

He didn't say anything. He just stood there with his arms crossed, looking away from her.

'I think it's too late,' he said, his voice all strained and tense.

'No! If I'm really sorry, it can't be too late,' Gina protested. She reached out for his arm and tried to slip her hand around it.

Dermot kept his arm pressed tightly to his side.

'Everyone knows about you and Callum,' he muttered. 'It's a bit humiliating.'

A bit?

Dermot's whole class was laughing at him and here he was calling it 'a bit' humiliating.

That was so sweet. So Dermot.

Gina's hand dropped from his arm.

'I'm so, so sorry,' she whispered, and she did really, truly mean it.

She would give anything for things to be back to normal again, for Dermot to have his arm around her and be telling her something funny.

The queue moved forward again, but this time Dermot stepped out of it.

'I don't think we're going to go and see this film, are

we?' he said. 'Despite the fact that it's a *"flawless allegory on modern capitalism"*.'

Gina shook her head. 'Could we go somewhere . . . to talk?'

Now Dermot shook his. 'I don't think so, Gina.'

Gina just stood there, still in the queue.

'Is this it?' she asked in a shaky voice.

Dermot's jaw was flicking again. She realized that he kept looking upwards because his eyes were watery, but he was determined not to cry.

'Dermot? Really? I'm sorry,' she pleaded. 'Look at me. I'm really, really sorry.'

But in a husky voice, he said, 'I need to be clear, Gina. I can't go out with someone who'd cheat on me with my friends. I need to be . . . clear.'

The lump in her throat had become hard and choking. 'I really liked you,' she heard herself blurt out, and she reached out to touch his rough tweedy coat sleeve.

Liked? She'd said 'liked' because she knew now that it was over.

He was about to walk away and not come back.

'I really liked you too.'

It sounded so final, it made her shiver.

'Please can I call you, Dermot? Later . . . maybe

next week?' she asked desperately, feeling her eyes well up now.

'I don't know.'

With that he turned, said a brief, 'Bye Gina,' and began to walk away.

Chapter Thirty-two

As soon as the phone bleeped in her handbag with a message, Gina slowed her tragic walk to the taxi rank and hurried to see who had texted her.

Could it be Dermot? Could he possibly have changed his mind?

She fumbled the phone out of her bag and took a look at the screen.

'HOW DID IT GO? ARE YOU FREE? CAL'

Gina was so annoyed by this, she actually let out a cry of frustration and stamped her foot.

'WHY NOT GO BUG YR GIRLFRIEND?' she texted back. Then she switched her phone off so that no matter what Callum replied, she wouldn't have to deal with it.

Gina had spent most of the past hour in a café on the phone to her mom; because there were some things that were so big, you just had to share with your mom.

Lorelei had been at a lunch party, but as soon as she'd worked out how upset Gina was, she'd excused herself from the crowd and gone to sit somewhere quiet to listen and sympathize.

'I can't tell you what to do . . . and I can't say what Dermot will do . . . or what will happen next,' Lorelei had told her kindly, 'but I can tell you, sweetheart, that even though this feels terrible now and like the worst thing that's ever happened, you will feel better soon. Your heart will mend. I promise you.'

In the back of the taxi back to the boarding house, Gina couldn't help thinking about Dermot: always so hard-working and cheerful in the café, always cracking jokes, making the best of that tiny bedroom in the tiny house he shared with his family. Didn't he always try to make the best of everything? Well, OK, except Charlie, maybe.

Dermot was a great person . . . and she'd blown it! She'd so totally blown it. For Callum . . . who had another girlfriend! Suddenly Gina found it impossible to stop crying.

But as the taxi rattled up Bute Gardens, she wiped her eyes and her nose, paid the fare, then walked slowly towards the front door, not wanting to go inside the boarding house until she had pulled herself together.

'Pssssssst! Gina?'

Gina looked around, not sure where the whisper had come from.

'Pssssssssssssssssst! Up here!'

Gina looked up. Now she could see Amy and Niffy's heads poking out of one of the upstairs windows.

'We're in Primrose dorm,' Amy said, still keeping her voice low. 'Come and see us.'

'Nah, I'm going to bed,' Gina replied.

'Just come,' Niffy added. 'We've got news.'

Gina went into the boarding house, signed the sheet in the sitting room, and spotted that only Miss McKinnon was on duty. Now she suspected the reason Niffy and Amy were on guard up at the window in Primrose.

'Good film?' Miss McKinnon asked.

'Erm . . . not bad,' Gina replied, desperate to get out of the room. 'I'm sorry, I've got a headache, I think I'll just go up to bed.'

'Oh dear, do you want me to get something from the medicine cupboard for you?'

'No, I'll be fine. I'll just get to bed early.'

'You look pale,' Miss McKinnon added. 'Just let me know if you need anything.'

'Thanks.'

With that Gina went out of the room and began to walk towards the dorm her friends were hanging out in. If she didn't go and see them, they would probably just come and find her anyway to bug her about what had happened.

'So, don't tell me – you're waiting for Mrs Knebworth to come back from her dinner date, right?' she asked as she pulled open the dorm door and saw Niffy and Amy crouching at the window in the dark. 'Why is this so interesting?'

'This is more than just friends,' Niffy answered. 'This is Mrs Knebworth having a *boyfriend* . . . it's big. It's Earth-shifting-on-its-axis stuff. It's unthinkable!'

Amy turned from the window and told Gina, 'We're probably just doing this stuff because we're bored. We didn't have nice cinema dates to go on tonight. How did Dermot take the bad news?'

At this question, Gina wilted and almost began to cry again.

'Oh dear . . .' Amy said. 'Sit down beside us and tell.'

Gina didn't think she wanted to, but somehow once she was squeezed between them, it was quite comforting to go through it all blow by blow. Their sympathy was very kind.

'That sounds hideous, horrible. You poor thing,' Amy soothed.

'Bit of a bummer that you changed your mind just as he decided he didn't want to hang around with you,' Niffy pointed out, earning herself a poke in the ribs from Amy.

'He knew about Callum!' Gina said, repeating the worst aspect of the entire evening. 'Callum has been showing people his phone photo of us kissing. It's so horrible.' She pressed her hands to her eyes to stop herself from crying.

Amy and Niffy exchanged a glance.

'Gina . . . we found out something about Callum,' Amy began. 'Just tonight. We'd have told you if we'd known before.'

'Yeah . . .' Niffy agreed.

Gina looked up and immediately guessed at what they were talking about.

'Dermot said Callum has a girlfriend in St Jude's . . . do you know who? Oh no . . . the card!'

She suddenly remembered Milly walking past her on

Valentine's Day and pointing out that they'd been sent the same card.

'It's Milly, isn't it?!'

'Yeah,' Niffy confirmed. 'Callum was the guy standing in the garden that night at the start of term.'

'Oh no . . .' Gina's lip wobbled dangerously. 'Does Milly know about me?'

'No,' Amy reassured her friend, putting an arm around her. 'I'm sorry, Gina. Breaking up is so horrible . . . and really upsetting. I should know. I've done it enough.'

'I don't want to break up with Dermot,' Gina said in a small, sad voice.

'Here comes Min,' Niffy said, her head still craned in the direction of the window, 'looking dreamy, her mind full of equations. Greg *plus* Min *over* cinema *times* popcorn *equals* love,' she joked.

Gina couldn't help pulling out her phone and switching it on . . . just to see, just to check if there was any word at all from Dermot.

Nothing.

'Why don't you phone him?' Amy said. 'Why don't you tell him that you don't want to break up?'

Gina shook her head.

'A text?' Amy suggested. 'C'mon, if you like him that

much, he has to be worth another shot. Go on . . . it can't make anything worse, can it?'

Gina looked at the phone in her hands.

'OK,' she agreed finally, then slowly and carefully tapped out the words: I AM SO SORRY. I DON'T WANT US TO BREAK UP. GINA XX

As she looked at them, totally unsure as to whether to send them or not, Amy leaned over and hit the Send button for her.

'Amy!' Gina stormed.

'That's what friends are for,' Amy replied with a smile.

'Give me your phone?' Niffy asked Gina.

'NO!' Gina replied, sure that Niffy was going to send Dermot something even worse.

'No, nothing to do with Dermot. I want to send a message to Angus.'

Gina handed the mobile over.

Niffy texted, reading the words aloud: HEY, ANGUS, GET FINN TO CALL AMY ASAP. TOTALLY OK WITH ME. NIFF XX

Despite the shriek of protest from Amy, Niffy hit Send before the phone could be wrestled from her hands.

'That's what friends are for,' Niffy said with a grin. Then, all of a sudden:

'Action stations. Headlights approaching driveway.'

'It'll just be another taxi . . . it's like Waverley Station out there at this time of night,' Amy said.

'No, no, up to the window.'

Gina saw the message symbol appear.

Dermot?

Callum?

Probably her mom leaving something cheerful and encouraging.

Her hand hovered over the button, but finally she pressed it.

SORRY 2. CALL ME. D XX

Gina couldn't help shrieking with excitement at this.

'Shhhhhh!' Niffy urged. 'Come over here.'

The three girls peering out through the window saw a big blue car pulling smoothly into the driveway at the front of the house.

'Action stations, action stations,' Niffy whispered. 'The Jaguar has landed. The Neb in festive floral frock is in the passenger's seat.'

All three watched, faces pressed to the glass, as Mrs Knebworth leaned over towards Jaguar man and, right there in front of their very eyes, illuminated by the bright interior light, Mrs K and Jaguar man puckered up and kissed each other long and hard on the lips.

'We've done this,' Amy whispered. 'We've driven her into his arms. It was our wine bottle . . .'

With a cheeky giggle, Niffy added: 'That's what friends are for.'

Read all the Secrets at St Jude's titles . . .

New Girl
by Carmen Reid

Ohmigod! Gina's mum has finally flipped and is sending her
to Scotland to some crusty old boarding school called St Jude's
– just because she spent all her money on clothes and got
a few bad grades! It's so unfair!

Now the Californian mall-rat has to swap her sophisticated
life of pool parties and well-groomed boys for hockey in
the rain, school dinners and stuffy housemistresses.
And what's with her three new dorm-buddies . . . could
they ever be her friends?

'Raucous, hilarious and heart-warming . . . Packed full
of friendship, fun, entertainment, love and hope'
www.lovereading.co.uk

ISBN: 978 0 552 55706 1

Jealous Girl
by **Carmen Reid**

Goodbye L.A., pools, malls and sunshine!

Hello Edinburgh, rain, hockey and school dinners!

Californian Gina is back in Scotland for a new term at
stuffy girls' school, St Jude's, and she's returned with
a secret jealousy.

But all the dorm girls have a reason to be jealous:
glamour-puss Amy is all green-eyed about Jason, swotty Min
longs to be like her cool friends and Niffy, stuck at home, is
jealous of everyone back at school.

The girls will have to stick together to make it
through this term!

ISBN: 978 0 552 55707 8

Drama Girl
by Carmen Reid

St Jude's – stuffy, dreary and dull? So wrong!
This term the dorm girls are in for some serious drama!

Gina can't wait for her mom and friends to visit.
But she's about to find out that mixing two sets
of best friends is trouble.

Niffy's brother wants to date Amy, but if that happens
Niffy's never going to talk to her again! Min wonders if
she will ever have the nerve to kiss her first boyfriend.
Meanwhile, Amy will do anything to look fabulous for
the school play, but she may be going too far.

Can the girls sort out their problems before
something *really* dramatic happens?

ISBN: 978 0 552 56121 1

My Desperate Love Diary
by Liz Rettig

There's G. Isn't he gorgeous? I think he just looked at me – well
he looked in my direction anyway. Do you think he'd ask me
out if I dyed my hair and got breast implants? *KELLY ANN*

I think you need brain implants, Kelly Ann, then maybe
you'd see what a complete idiot G is. *STEPHANIE*

Stephanie's right. OK, G's not ugly but he's SO up
himself! You'd be much better off with Chris. He's
gorgeous and crazy about you, if only you'd
open your eyes . . . *LIZ*

Don't be stupid! Chris is a good friend but that's it. I'd rather
snog my brother (if I had one). Now be serious, how do I get
G to notice me? A blonde wig and a Wonderbra? *KELLY ANN*

Read the hilarious and excruciating diary of Kelly Ann,
a teenage girl who wants bigger boobs, blonder hair – and
the biggest idiot in school to fall in love with her . . .

'Heartfelt but at the same time fantastically funny,
this is a holiday must-read' *Mizz*

ISBN: 978 0 552 55332 2

Split by a Kiss
by Louisa Plaja

I'm two different people. Literally. I'm split.

Jo has never been one of the popular kids . . . until she
moves to the USA. Suddenly the coolest girls at her new
high school adopt her, and the hottest boy, Jake Matthews,
notices her. But when Jake picks her as his partner in
the kissing game Seven Minutes in Heaven, it's not half
as heavenly as she imagined!

Jo has a choice: should she carry on going with Jake for
guaranteed popularity – or should she tell him where to
get off and risk losing her new friends . . . ?

At this moment Jo splits. She's Josie the Cool – girlfriend
of Jake, member of the in-crowd. But she's also
Jo the Nerd – rejected by the It girls, single . . . ordinary.
Will her two halves ever come together again?

ISBN: 978 0 552 55680 4